BUGS FROM THE PAST

NITHISH G MADHAV

Contents

Contents

Contents

The Baggage of Another Man

CHAPTER ONE

After a night of tormented sleep, he died a human being and is now reborn as a giant bug. He opens his eyes with a start and gasps. He breathes hoarsely, but there is something insect-like about the sound of his breath. He tries to get up, but his body weight pulls him back. He tilts his face down and looks at his body, at the two hands that have grown out of either sides of his abdomen. He wants this to end as a nightmare. But it is not. He feels a sharp pain running through his chest, maybe his heart, if bugs had a heart. He doesn't know much about a bug's body. He resented bugs to begin with, and now he finds himself as one.

The thoughts that come to him feel incomprehensible. They feel like the descriptions of a nightmare. "Wake up..." he whispers to himself, as if he's still sleeping. But he is not. His eyes are open, and he had seen the weird body and moving limbs.

Although he is in a struggle with himself to get his back off the bed, he can hear the voices calling his name out. Maybe it is someone, probably his mother, asking him to get up, because despite everything else, he knows that he is getting late. Maybe it is someone who has come straight out of the nightmares he was having in the last night. He does not seem to understand anything.

There is a sound at the door, and Gregor tilts his face towards it. The door isn't locked from the inside. The handle goes down, the door is opened and a pair of eyes peeps in. Gregor can barely see the door, and he doesn't know who opened it. His vision is almost a blur. The door is then opened wide, and a young woman, his sister, rushes into the room and runs towards his side. Gregor is out of words. He feels embarrassed. He wishes that he had locked the door last night so that his sister would not have seen him in this state. He wants to open his mouth and say something, but no voice comes forth.

She now sits by the side of his bed and has her arm around his body. She shakes body, as if he is unconscious. But that doesn't wake him up from the dream he is supposedly having.

She calls out for her mother, who is working in the kitchen. The last thing Gregor wants is more people in the room. He shakes his head, trying to convey these thoughts to his sister, but she clearly does not comprehend it. "He is not feeling well," she shouts. There is some sudden noise in the kitchen, like a utensil has fallen down. Gregor barely hears this. It feels like some distant sound in a nightmare to him. Immediately, both of Gregor's parents assemble in the room, along with his sister. They stand at three different points of his vision. One rubs on his head, the others massage on his hands, abdomen and thighs. "Calm... down..." The voices are mixed and muffled in his head, like they all came from a single person. "He... has... oh... never... felt... God... young... What's... happening..." He can't comprehend anything.

There are just words and words, jumbled on top of each other. He wants to tell his parents that they shouldn't worry, that they shouldn't get involved in his problems, and that he can solve these problems all by himself. Since Gregor had started earning for his family, he had started seeing himself as a self-sufficient man who could take care of himself and his family no matter what. But now he is appearing weak. He should be taking care of his father and mother and now the opposite happens. He wanted to ask them to leave and let him be alone and allow him to manage everything by himself. But neither he had the voice nor he had the physical ability to shove them away.

Gregor's phone rings on the bedside table, where it was plugged in. Gregor makes noises, wanting to take the call himself. But Gregor's sister already has her hand on it. "It's his boss," she says to her parents, who are already in a state of despair. "Should I take the phone?" She asks her parents with a frown.

"Take the phone, and tell them what is happening," the mother says, wiping tears off her face.

His sister takes the phone, and even the parents can hear the voice of the manager from the other end, who is shouting, thinking that the person who took the phone was Gregor.

"Excuse me, sir. It's his sister," she says, surprisingly in a calm tone. If it wasn't her brother's manager, then she would have shouted back at him and ended up in tears. "Sir, he is not feeling well. We just came to check on him as he didn't wake up on time. He seems to be having a seizure... No sir, I am not lying. Why would I lie that my dear brother is having a seizure?... Yes sir, we also know that Gregor is a healthy person, and even we are confused why he is acting weirdly now... We need to be patient, sir. I don't know about that, sir. I will call you, or I will ask my brother to call you back, when everything is fine here... Yes sir... Sure... Thank you..."

The young woman sighs as she cuts the call. "That guy thinks that everyone is a machine, except him. He can't even comprehend the fact that my brother is sick and he is late for work. He talks like, *How can machines get seizures? I only serviced it last week.* He also thinks that my brother is putting on a show because he was being dishonest at work these days. How is that possible? He is the most simple and honest person I have ever seen."

Gregor still cannot conjoin the voices he hears with what is happening around him and within himself. He is still seeing the body of a bug and the flailing limbs when he looks down, and his parents and sister are getting hold of it, showing no sign of disgust or discomfort, trying to soothe him.

"Calm down. Calm down."

"Son..."

"He hasn't been like this in twenty years. I don't know what got to him now."

"Relax. This seizure will stop. Let's stay with him till then."

"He used to have seizures when he was young."

"We should find a good doctor."

"Gregor doesn't like hospitals."

"Nobody likes hospitals. Neither do I."

The family is talking, and all these voices conjoin in his head, loudly, into one static sound. The sound gets louder and louder, and for Gregor, it feels as if his ears will burst. For a moment, Gregor forgets that he was a bug who couldn't get his back up from the bed. He wakes up as if from a dream, gets up, and sits straight on his bed, exhaling forcefully as if he is being exorcised. He feels human presence around him and sees three people. He stares at them as if they were aliens, or maybe as if he were one. It takes him a minute or two to reorient himself. He remembers how he went to sleep like a human being last night, just like the people who are around staring at him with anticipation. The horrifying image he saw a few minutes ago was nothing but a fleshed-out nightmare—it wasn't real, but more real than reality itself.

Gregor looks at his mother, who is wiping off tears. His father's face looks worried and emotional, and his sister's face doesn't give away any feeling. She looks at Gregor with a blank face.

"Are you okay?" His mother asked.

Gregor nods. He sighs, as if forgetting himself in the beauty of living and of breathing. He looks at everything as if he had died and is reborn.

His mother gets up, kisses him on his forehead, and leaves the room. His father, who was standing to his right, taps firmly on his shoulder and leaves too. His sister joins them after giving him an inscrutable look. After they leave, Gregor buries his head in between his knees and covers his head with his hands. His sister returns to the door and watches him silently. Gregor notices her presence and looks up. She smiles warmly.

"Is my eye red in colour?" He says, pointing at his left eye.

"Yes." She nods.

"It hurts," he says, covering his face like an annoyed child.

A few weeks ago, Gregor woke up with a sharp pain in his eye. He looked in the mirror to find his left eye bloodshot. Gregor spent the whole day thinking that he was slowly losing his eyesight. He even thought about how he had taken his eyesight for granted, and that day he had promised himself to take better care of his eyes, in whatever time he had left. His thoughts finally dissolved when, to his relief, his eyes looked perfectly normal the next morning.

Gregor had never shared any of these seemingly silly little worries with anyone in his life. In fact, he had never shared anything with anyone. Even his parents don't know how much he resented bugs and how much they have haunted him throughout his life. When he was trying to live a life built by distractions, the bugs have found their way back.

If you see Gregor, you can always see a silent person unable to express whatever is going on inside him and trying in vain to hide it with a smile; trying in vain to act strong.

CHAPTER TWO

Gregor stares into the mirror, looking deep into his reflection. He doesn't feel like brushing his teeth or taking a bath. His gaze lingers on his red, bloodshot eye, and his face, which has grown pale and haggard. The longer he looks, the more he fears his face will morph into the grotesque head of a giant bug—long antennae, compound eyes, feelers, and jaws staring back at him, ready to devour him whole if given the chance. His face betrays the evidence of tears and the attempts to wash them away. He examines his red eye, wondering how to reduce the angry colour. He washes his face repeatedly, splashing water into his eye, but it only seems to worsen the redness. He remembers the last time his eye was red; how he had searched the internet for answers, but found nothing helpful. A sharp, familiar pain pulses through his chest, echoing the one he had felt earlier in bed. He tears his gaze away from the mirror and turns to the toothbrush stand. Mechanically, he applies toothpaste to the brush and begins brushing his teeth, staring blankly into the mirror. As he does, he catches a glimpse of a bug clinging to his eye. Panic flares before he realizes he's hallucinating. He smacks the side of his head and looks away, trying to shake the image from his mind.

The vision brings back memories of the previous evening, on the train ride back home. He recalls sitting next to a man who had his eyes covered with a piece of cloth, constantly dabbing at them as if in pain. But Gregor had barely noticed the man; he rarely paid attention to anyone around him. He was too preoccupied with his phone, mindlessly scrolling through Instagram reels and news videos on YouTube, lost in the digital distractions he clung to so desperately.

"What happened to your eyes?" Someone asked this man.

"Oh, it's a bug."

This caught Gregor's attention, and for the first time, he looked at the man sitting next to him. The cloth no longer covered the man's eye, revealing a disturbing wound. The eye was swollen to the size of a large stone, with a raw, pink wound glaring at its centre. The swelling had reduced the eye to a narrow slit, so small that the man could barely see through it.

"A few days back, I was walking through the forest, and a bug fell on my eye. I didn't know how to deal with it. Kerosene or even salt would've helped. But, I came to know about it later. My friend plucked the bug away from my eye and just threw it away. I had pain in my eye throughout the day, and it intensified at night. I had my wife check my eye, and she told me she found the bug's jaw was still stuck inside. She took it out and my eyes started swelling the next day. It had gotten better. But yesterday I got the wound exposed to dust and it got worse, and now I'm on my way back from the hospital."

Gregor had tried not to listen to that man. He had only heard bits and pieces. He was instead looking at his phone, and trying to get occupied in it. But since then, Gregor started having pain in his eye, which then spread to other parts of his head. He was feeling nauseous, so he skipped dinner that night and went straight to bed.

CHAPTER THREE

"You don't have to go if you are not feeling perfect," his mother says, as she pours curry onto his plate.

Gregor just shakes his head, as if not interested in small talk. He wants to tell his mother that it has been years since he had felt "perfect". His mind is filled with office work. He knows that he is already late, and he must make haste. He will definitely have to confront the boss and endure whatever he has to tell him. He must listen to it like a deaf guy, do his work properly, and take care of his family.

"At least visit a doctor on your way back."

Gregor shakes his head and says irritatedly. "Okay, I will. Please let me have this first."

But the moment those words leave his mouth, he instantly feels guilty of his tone. So he just stands up, having eaten almost nothing, and goes to pack his bag, ignoring his mother's questioning gaze. He hurriedly grabs his lunchbox and water bottle from his mother before heading out the door. This time, he leaves without his usual smile for her, something he only realizes while on the train. Moments spent looking at the world going behind were always a moment of contemplation for him. He feels guilty for an instant. He remembers something he once heard. Never leave anyone without a smile. Maybe it's the last time you're seeing them. Suddenly he wants to go back in time and leave the house with a warm smile. It is not possible now. He doesn't want to go to work. But when the train stops, he has to get up and put on a show, be someone who is not himself. Be someone who doesn't have "no" for an answer. Play a key role in a routine one-act play that runs for almost ten hours.

As Gregor exits the railway station, a small boy, no more than two or three years old, comes running toward him with no sense of direction. The child nearly collides with him, but Gregor gently stops him by placing his hands on the boy's shoulders. The boy is dressed in shabby, torn clothes, and his face is smudged with dirt, yet there's a certain beauty in his innocent eyes.

The boy's mother, also dressed in worn, shabby clothes, stands nearby, engrossed in a loud conversation on her phone. Gregor pauses for a moment, looking into the boy's eyes, feeling an inexplicable connection.

"Boy, you'll get red eyes too!" the mother suddenly shouts as she pulls the boy by his wrist, away from Gregor. She continues talking loudly on her phone as she heads into the railway station.

Gregor watches them for a brief moment, then quickly turns and hurries toward his office.

CHAPTER FOUR

It is twenty minutes past noon, and Gregor is already feeling hungry, for he has eaten near to nothing for breakfast. Gregor spends time with more pretence than actually doing his work. He needs to crunch away forty more minutes for the lunch break. He thinks about the lunch that his mother packs for him. It is always the same lunch every day with little to no differences. It has started losing its taste. He realises that this normal lunch will not satisfy his hunger. Maybe he should order something in. But he chooses not to, because firstly, the lunch his mother packed will go to waste, and secondly, if he is ordering for himself, then he will have to order something for his co-workers as well. It is almost impossible for him to have special food all by himself in this office. So, in the end, he chooses to go with the normal lunch, without any complaints. For a moment he becomes, at least for himself, a Good Samaritan, who understands the value of food.

Forty minutes crawl by, and Gregor feels like he has already seen a year pass by. He sits at his table and places his plastic lunch box on top, surrounded by colleagues settling in at near and far tables. He doesn't like to interact with anyone while having lunch. People are only starting to settle in, and as Gregor is someone who waits for none when it comes to food, takes his lunch box in his hand and tries to open it. But, he can't. He tries a little harder, but it still won't turn. He tries harder, with all his might, and he starts receiving awkward glances from his colleagues. He hits the lunch box on the table and on the floor, trying his best not to invite any attention and it still won't open up. Gregor realises that it is something he cannot do. The man sitting next to him offers help. Without knowing what else to do, Gregor passes the lunch box to him. He tries his best, but the lunch box remains the same. He indicates to Gregor that he can't do it. The man gives the lunch box back to Gregor, who tries a little more, again hits it on the floor, and tries to open it, but nothing works. By then, others start noticing him, and suddenly everyone wants to help him. A man with a well-built body asks Gregor to pass the lunch box to him. He tries with all his might, all in vain. The well-built guy passes the lunch box to the guy next to him, and then to the next guy, and almost everyone in that room tries to open the lunch box with no luck. The lunch box finally returns in the hands of the owner, who again tries to open it. His stomach burns and feels as if he is losing his eyesight. Everything is a blur, as he tries to look at his lunchbox and work on it. But, it doesn't open. By then, it has become a common issue among the group. All eyes are on the lunch box. The well-built man asks for the lunch box again. Gregor passes it. He tries again. He tries with another guy sitting next to him. They attempt to pry it open with four hands. But still, the lunch box does not even turn a millimetre.

"It seems impossible," the well-built man says, as he tries even harder. Everyone is now a spectator to that sport, and it seems as if the person who opens it, will receive the status of a hero.

The lunch box takes another round among the employees, and it finally reaches back to the hands of the well-built guy.

"We need a conclusion to this. It's not as if we can never open this lunch box," he says and looks at Gregor. "Do you mind if I break this?"

Gregor shakes his head.

The well-built man starts with determination, as he begins to work again. He tries to turn the lunch box, he hits it harder on the floor as if he had the intention to break it. He goes again and again, harder and harder. Finally the box breaks and the contents of the lunch box spill on the floor. Gregor hears claps and cheers around him. Some people appreciate the guy. He passes the opened lunch box to Gregor. "I'm sorry, you lost most of it, but something remains."

Gregor shakes his head, doesn't smile or say thank you and gets his lunch back from the guy. He eats the remaining food and gets up to wash his hands. He behaves as if none of these have bothered him, although he is a hungry and disjointed mess on the inside.

CHAPTER FIVE

Gregor recalls the last time he stayed late at work, two months ago. He had been assigned some urgent tasks just as he was about to wrap up for the day. That night, he didn't leave until seven, an hour later than usual. His regular train was long gone, so he had to wait another forty minutes for the next one. Surprisingly, the train was less crowded than usual, which made Gregor consider staying late every day. He found a seat and, for once, didn't pull out his phone. Instead, he stared out into the darkness, finding an unusual sense of peace where he normally sought distraction.

When the train reached his station, Gregor disembarked and began the walk home. It was a moonless night, and the streets were already quiet and deserted. As he approached an isolated corner, something caught his eye to the left—a group of teenage boys. They were surprisingly silent, and when they saw Gregor, their expressions turned to shock. Gregor, who usually avoided getting involved in others' affairs, felt a sense of suspicion. Something about the scene unsettled him, and he suspected that drugs might be the reason for their gathering. He paused a few meters away from them, watching closely. Then, he noticed a girl of their age standing at the center of the group, looking terrified. The boys, too, seemed uneasy, their faces betraying a mix of guilt and fear. Without thinking, Gregor walked closer to them. "What are you guys doing here?" he asked, his voice steady despite the tension in the air.

"Nothing," one of the boys said casually, shrugging, as if it was enough to make Gregor leave. But he stayed there with more resolution, looking inquisitively at the teenagers.

"What is it in your hands?" Gregor asked, pointing at the folded newspaper one of the boys carried.

"It's just a newspaper," the boy said, keeping it away from Gregor.

"So you've joined here to listen to the evening news?" Gregor said. The teenagers were silent. "Give that newspaper to me."

"Who are you to ask that? That's none of your business," another boy snapped from the opposite side. Before Gregor could respond, the first attack came. A stone, thrown with force, struck the side of his head. The impact was sudden and jarring, knocking him off balance and sending him to the ground. Gregor instinctively reached up to the spot where the stone had hit. His fingers brushed against the warm, thick liquid already seeping from the wound. Blood.

"Let's finish off this guy!" one of the boys shouted, his voice dripping with malice. Gregor barely had time to register the threat before he felt the brutal pressure of a boot grinding into his upper arm. The pain shot through him, but before he could react, a hard slap landed across his face, so forceful that his vision blurred. The sting of the blow resonated through his skull, and for a moment, he was certain some of his teeth had been knocked loose.

"Let him go," the girl cried.

Gregor struggled to stand, his limbs trembling under the weight of pain and shock, but he collapsed back onto the ground. From that low vantage point, the world looked different—alien, almost. He saw the shoes of the teenagers moving away, and as they departed, his eyes focused on the tiny stones and grains of sand scattered across the ground. It was a strange perspective, one he had never experienced before, as if seeing the world from a new, unfamiliar angle. Lying on his back, Gregor watched as the group of teenagers finally disappeared from his view, leaving him alone with the quiet night and the cold, unforgiving earth beneath him.

That night when his mother inquired what happened to him, Gregor said he just fell down, and dodged all other questions that came his way. Gregor spent days and nights taking revenge against them in his thoughts and dreams. But he never tried to take efforts to actually confront them.

Amid the scary thoughts springing from hunger and fatigue, the thoughts about those teenagers also come to him. He looks at his watch and back at the computer screen. Gregor is asked to stay late as a punishment for arriving late this morning. In the morning when his boss berated him, he only said "sorry" because the explanation was already given by his sister in that phone call, and there was nothing more for him to say. But that didn't stop his boss from using the opportunity to find every possible fault with him throughout the day, punctuating each tirade with the usual threat: "I don't want you to stay. You can quit if you want to!"

People pass by and through him like ghosts. As he stands at the railway station, scrolling through Instagram reels he does not seem to realise how haunted everything feels like. His hunger has by then become a part of his being. Maybe he is tired of feeling hungry. He tries not to think about food, particularly not anything tasty. Gregor had already made plans to buy something that he liked, from the restaurant which was near his home. When his colleagues go to the canteen to have some tea and snacks, Gregor will be the only one who stayed back at his table and continued with his work. Today, he wanted to go with them, but whenever he looked at his boss, the big fat man always had his eyes on him, which refused him to even move a little. Today was the day Gregor really considered quitting his job. What refuses him is the state of uncertainty and depression he was in, three years ago. It is not that his job is not giving him enough and maybe plenty of chances to feel anxious and depressed. But, the office helps in distracting himself from these thoughts. Also the office provides him a change of setting, and ofcourse, ultimately, money.

Gregor scrolls through Instagram reels and eventually lands on the video of a guy singing. The singer is somewhat of a celebrity online, and as Gregor listens to the song, he finds it soothing, calming his nerves. He glances at the comments, noticing that many people seem to share the same feelings he's experiencing. The music blares out of his phone's stereo since he isn't using earphones. Curious, he clicks on the singer's profile and discovers that the artist also plays the violin. Gregor is so absorbed in the song that he doesn't notice a man standing right by his shoulder.

"Got you!" The man says. It is right beside his ear and Gregor is spooked.

"Godammit! Who are you!" Gregor turns to his right and sees the man clearly illuminated by the lights in the railway station. The brightness of the colours in his flowery shirt is a bit darkened by the darkness of the night. He had a bag on his back, which was used to carry musical instruments, like violin and guitar. Gregor thinks for ten seconds like where has he seen him before. The man is looking at him with a big smile, and a surprised face. It immediately dawns upon him.

"Oh God! Are you this guy?" Gregor asks, pointing at his phone and his face glows slowly into a wide smile.

"Yes." The man nods, still managing that surprised smile.

"You know, I was about to write a comment underneath your song. But now there's no need for that. I can tell you directly."

"Oh what were you planning to write?"

"Oh, it's nothing. I was just planning to give a face filled with love emoji."

"Just that?"

"Just that," Gregor says. "But now that I got you in life and blood, I've a lot to tell you."

"It feels good, you know? To randomly see someone listening to my song, and liking it. Infact, it feels great."

"But tell me," Gregor says. "How can you even sing like this? I listened to your songs, and I suddenly felt like my problems were vanishing. It's such a cathartic experience. Your voice is a gift of God."

The man laughs. "I'm grateful to hear that. What was your name again?"

"Oh I didn't introduce myself. Gregor."

The musician tells his name.

"What do you do, Gregor?" He then asks.

"Well, there's nothing glorious about my life."

The musician studies Gregor for a second. There is silence.

"Whatever I do, it's not what I want to do with my life, you know?"

"Then, what do you want to do?"

"I don't know about that either. I just hate my life. Like, real hate."

"Would you believe I hate my life, too?" The Musician says, and he moves closer to Gregor. "Gregor, it's not the circumstances that need to be changed. It's us."

Gregor nods. This guy is not just someone who can impress you with his songs, but also with his words.

"What is it that troubles you?" The Musician asks.

The siren of the train blares, and it arrives at the station. Gregor and the musician walk into the bogie. The train is almost empty, so they sit on opposite seats.

"You know, even my doctor has never asked me this question"

"You have a doctor?" The musician asks, suddenly. "What are you suffering from?"

"I used to have seizures when I was young."

"So, you remember the words of a doctor that you met years back."

"Bro I was just making a joke, to help you understand that that question was never asked to me by anyone."

"Oh, calm down, dear Gregor."

"I am calm," Gregor says with a sudden smile. "What made you think that I am not?"

"Forgive me. Forget I said that."

"Why are you asking for my forgiveness?" By now, Gregor understands how every conversation that he is involved in, automatically gets weird. He then adds, "I don't have to forgive you. Instead, I think I should say sorry for raising my voice."

"Oh, no, Gregor. Please, it's alright."

Gregor smiles apologetically, and looks outside the train window. The train is now passing through a tunnel, and the window gets darker and the sound of the train gets louder.

Probably a minute passes before The Musician speaks. "Could you believe that I'm having an emotional breakdown right now?"

Gregor turns towards him, stunned at the sudden words that came out of nowhere. Instead of speaking anything, Gregor looks at the musician with a brief smile that seems to encourage him to talk more. But that smile makes the man nothing else but uncomfortable.

"It's been months since I properly slept. Do you know why I still sing?"

Gregor shakes his head.

"Because it's the only thing that keeps me alive."

"What is it that bothers you?" Gregor asks.

"I don't want to bore you with my life," he says with a smile. "No, I was asking you the same question. You can't UNO reverse me."

"What is that?" Gregor asks.

"Just answer my question instead of avoiding it."

"You know what? I don't want to bore you with my life either."

"I must admit that I'm bored already," the musician says in low volume. "Fine, you win. I'll tell you my story." The man says.

"So, are you going to tell me your life story now?" Gregor says, and sits straight, as if preparing himself to listen.

"Yes."

"Go on. I'm listening."

"At 21, I had everything in my life. A girlfriend who was with me for thirteen long years, a moderately supportive family, a career worth pursuing, confidence - maybe too much of it. I was the strongest man, you know? When I was 22, my girlfriend who was of my age, asked me if we could get married. I said no. I wanted to be free. But you know, breaking the heart of that one person who loves you the most, is one of the worst things you can ever do. Even if you believe in Karma or not, it'll haunt you very badly.

"I said no, and my life started declining from there, at least in the background. I didn't stop working hard. Wanted to make it big as a singer. Nothing was particularly happening in my family. A drunk father, a sad and diseased mother, a busy brother. I was almost never at home. Always traveling in pursuit of music. And that's when my father died. And fuck, didn't that hurt like hell?

"You know, I was not friendly with my father, we fought almost everytime we came face to face, so we always tried to avoid a confrontation. But his death was like a mighty slap on my face. To say I was depressed would be an understatement. I went through therapy and I got a bit normal. After that, I fell in love again, with a girl who was already in love with someone - a detail I came to know a bit late. Ofcourse, it wasn't reciprocated, infact I didn't even confess my love for her. My mother and music were my only lifeline.

"I was striving so hard to breathe properly everyday. Although I was with people, everyone only seemed like a different form of loneliness, and all these different forms of loneliness were surrounding me, suffocating me. And then one day, six months back, the unthinkable happened. My mother died. I was finished. I was done. I started crying every night and put this smile on me when the dark night brightens." The musician says. There is no trace of sadness in his face. He smiles like someone who is so happy and satisfied with his life. Smile is, indeed, the most beautiful lie.

"You know what, my problems seem like nothing in front of yours."

The musician shakes his head. "Everyone lives a tough life, you know? No one is happy in this fucking world. The life of every individual is important. The struggle of every individual is important. So, what you go through is serious, if it's affecting you so much."

"It is affecting me so much."

"There you go."

"While what bothers you is outside of yourself, what bothers me is inside. Inside my mind. I was born with a derailed mind, you know?"

"Don't use such stupid words on a train, dude," the musician says, laughing.

"I was wondering if you can sing a song for me." Gregor says.

"Only if you tell me your life story. You know, be a gentleman. You just heard my story."

Gregor nods. "Sure then."

"But hold on," the musician says. "I think I'll have to empty my bladder first."

Gregor just nods as he watches the musician stand up and leave towards the end of the bogie.

"Bladder first."

Gregor feels sleepy and tired as the cold December winds whisper through the cracks of the train. The chill is biting but not unbearable—just enough to make him long for the warmth of sleep. He struggles to keep his eyes open, but they remain half-closed, and soon, he drifts into a dream. In his dream, Gregor sees The Musician sitting opposite him, strumming a guitar and singing a song he adores. The melody is captivating, and the musician is lost in it, singing with a self-indulgent joy that makes the song even more beautiful. Gregor marvels at the scene, thinking how much better the day has become. The morning was filled with pain, hurt, insults, and punishments, yet here he is now, comfortably seated by the window of the train, listening to an amazing musician play his favorite song. Life, in this moment, feels perfect.

But something is off. As Gregor watches the musician, he notices subtle changes in his appearance. His facial features begin to shift—where is the beard that had framed his face? Why does he suddenly look chubbier? The shirt with flowers is gone, replaced by an orange t-shirt. Gregor's heart sinks as he realizes something is wrong. This isn't real. He is dreaming.

He wakes up with a start, his heart pounding. The berth opposite him is empty, save for The Musician's bags. Gregor glances around, trying to shake off the remnants of the dream. People usually spend a long time in the toilet, though Gregor never understands why—he is always in and out in less than a minute. "Let him take his time," Gregor thinks as he looks out the window, fighting the urge to fall asleep again.

After nearly fifteen minutes, Gregor grows restless. He stands up and decides to check the toilet. The door is open, and the small space is empty. The water closet stares back at him, blank and indifferent, offering nothing in return.

As he makes his way back, Gregor notices the musician standing by the open train door, exhaling a cloud of smoke into the cold air. The musician turns and smiles at him, but Gregor's face remains expressionless. The dream has shattered something inside him, leaving him with an emptiness he can't quite place.

"Sorry I got a call. I was attending it, and then I thought I should smoke," the man laughs lightly.

"You shouldn't stand here."

"Yeah. It's alright. You know, I like it."

Gregor stands opposite to him and watches him smoke. Gregor then moves a little away, so that the smoke will not reach him. Gregor never liked the smell of it.

"You know, someone messaged me from the movie industry, after listening to my songs on Instagram," he says smiling.

Gregor's face brightens into a smile. "That's a great thing, bro."

"Yeah. But, that was two days back. Now that guy has called me again. He said it's not going to happen. They got another guy to do the job." There is a genuine sadness on his face.

Gregor wanted to pat his shoulders or give him a hug. But he doesn't, because of the smoke. Gregor instead nods, as if to let him know that he has listened to what he has just said.

"You know what, I'll manage. It's part of life, right? I mean, I've been through bigger and harder times, and this is just..." he stops and looks outside. Gregor watches him with a face that betrays concern. "Just a small thing you know." Without warning, the musician hurls himself out of the speeding train. His body strikes a pole with a sickening crunch, the sound reverberating like a death knell.

Gregor stands paralyzed, the horror of what he's witnessed rooting him to the spot. Then, as if a bolt of electricity jolts through him, he collapses to the floor. He clutches his face with trembling hands, desperate to scream, but no sound escapes his throat. Only silence, thick and suffocating, envelops him. Curling into himself, Gregor buries his face between his knees, his mind teetering on the brink of madness. He can't shake the image of the musician's broken body, the lifeless thud echoing in his ears.

Finally, he forces himself to stand, feeling as if he's moving through a nightmare. His eyes catch his reflection in a small mirror on the opposite wall. Staring back at him is not his face, but the visage of an insect, its beady eyes and chitinous skin glistening with malice. A cold shudder runs down his spine as the thought creeps into his mind, like a whisper: *Maybe he saw my insect head. Maybe that's why he jumped.*

Gregor returns to his seat, his mind still reeling from what he had just witnessed. His eyes lock onto the baggage placed above the berth opposite him—the travel bag and the one with the violin. Something about them feels ominous now, as if they carry the weight of the happenings of that evening. Without hesitation, he grabs the bags, and bolts down the narrow aisle. He races through the swaying train cars, his only thought being to reach the railway police station.

Unoriginal Experiences

CHAPTER SIX

In the dreams, Gregor sees a giant caterpillar crawling into his mouth. He could feel its slow, deliberate movement as it slid down his food canal, finally reaching his stomach where it got stuck, unsure of where to go next. The creature began to explore, its tiny legs brushing against the lining of his stomach, sending waves of tickling discomfort through his body. The sensation grew stronger, more intense, until it jolted him awake. Gregor remembers the dream for a fraction of a second. In the dream, he was not himself, he was the caterpillar.

Gregor gets up from his bed and looks down at his body. It is the body of a normal human being. Gregor sighs, passes by the corridor to his room, sees his parents and sister already awake, and goes into the bathroom. He stands there before the mirror, and studies his face. He leans in closer and sees the long antennas sprouting from his forehead, becoming clearer and more defined. He reaches up to touch them. He doesn't get the touch sensation in his hand, but in the mirror, the antennas are real and his hand is actually touching them. He stops looking at the mirror and starts brushing his teeth.

Last night, after returning home late from the police station, Gregor got a call from a friend who he had not spoken to in over a decade. It was well past 1 AM, and Gregor was struggling to fall asleep. All his thoughts revolved around the experience he had in the train just a few hours back. Gregor took the call just because he had nothing else to do. His mind was in a state of unrest, in a state of chaos, and he desperately wanted something to calm himself down. Gregor also wondered why this old friend was calling him at this absurd hour.

He usually kept his phone on silent mode, but tonight was different. He had turned the volume up, expecting a call from the police station with updates about the musician. After giving the authorities all the information he had, they had sent him home, promising to contact him if they learned anything new.

The phone rang loudly on the bedside table, its sharp tone cutting through the stillness of the night. Gregor reached for it immediately, and attended the call.

"Hello," Gregor said.

"You didn't sleep?"

"No."

The man laughed from the other end. Gregor listened to this without any change of expression, but also had a million calculations in his mind as to why he called.

"Do you remember me?"

"Yeah. I do."

"I honestly didn't remember you, until now; until now when I saw your name in my contact list. I called you immediately because I might forget it later, you get me?"

"Oh. I understand," Gregor says, "But I do remember you perfectly. Very vividly indeed."

"God, I wish I had your memory, you know?" The man said and started laughing in loud volume. "You know these medicines and pills are seeing the better of me."

Listening to another sad story was the last thing he wanted at that moment, so he did not inquire further.

"Gregor, why are you so silent now? Is it your life experiences?"

"I have always been silent."

"Oh. I don't remember much about you. I don't even remember much about myself, for that matter. But I do remember someone who was so volatile and always trying to make people laugh by being a joker. Was that you? Or am I remembering it wrong?"

Gregor paused, the question hanging in the air. He let the silence linger as he sifted through his memories, searching for a version of himself that matched his friend's description. It felt like peeling away layers, seeing his life for what it truly was, without any comforting illusions.

"Why are you not saying anything?"

"What should I say?"

"I was asking if that was you, or am I remembering it wrong?"

"You are remembering it wrong."

Thus, Gregor plucked away the memories about himself from a man whose mind was deteriorating.

"Alright..." the man said. "Alright... It's impossible to trust my mind these days. Forgive me. But I'm sure, there used to be a guy like that in our school, you remember?"

"Yeah," Gregor said, and mentioned the name of his only friend during school days. He could feel the memories flood back, unbidden and sharp. Gregor was the one who had been volatile, always acting the fool in class, doing random, impulsive things just to get a reaction. His friend had always been there, tagging along, supporting him, imitating him, trying to be like him. Gregor remembered how he used to relish creating the worst image of himself, presenting it to others just to be insulted, laughed at, and even abused. The man on the other end of the line had been one of those who followed him, bullying him. "Insect... insect..." that was Gregor's nickname. They said he looked like one—thin body, small head, long limbs. At some point, Gregor realized that this behavior was doing him no good, only harm. He stopped acting out and started focusing on his studies instead. When Gregor was a young boy, all he wanted was to enjoy every bit of his youth, making use of every second, wanting to entertain others, even if it meant making a fool of himself. But then, life happened.

"Who is that? I don't remember him," the man said.

"Maybe one day you will remember him like how you remembered me."

"Maybe I'll. Fuck my memory, you know."

"No. It's actually a blessing. To forget things."

Memories of the musician jumping off the train flashed in his mind. Gregor had wanted so much to find someone who understood him, but instead, he was left alone once more, with nothing but the remnants of a conversation and the haunting image of a man disappearing into the night.

"Why didn't you pull the chain?" That was the first question the police officer asked when Gregor had explained the whole thing to him. The officer was raging, and behaved as if he would slap him. "It could've saved his life. If he dies, consider it your fault."

Gregor felt like someone was trying to choke him using metal wires. Thoughts clouded his brain like a rainy day. He was looking back at the fan, rotating, like to the tunes of a spiralling music. He put the phone to his side, without disconnecting it. Tear drops started tracing the side of his face. The voice of his old bully, now distant and indistinct, continued to drone on. Gregor could barely register the words; they felt like echoes from a past he wanted to forget. The call was disconnected after sometime, and another call came to his phone. He picked the phone up. It was the police officer who had talked to him before.

"Hello... sir..." Gregor said, his voice breaking.

"Gregor, you'll have to report to the police station tomorrow."

"Sure sir, I will."

"And, we found his dead body."

Gregor was silent. He didn't know what to say, and whatever thoughts that came to his mind, didn't get simplified into words, and the words that formed in his mind, didn't come forth in a proper sentence.

"Gregor...? Gregor...? Are you alright?" The police officer said from the other end. "Gregor, please don't take what I said before seriously. This death is not your fault. It's not. I'm sorry for what I said. It's not your fault."

"Ok sir," Gregor responded. "I haven't taken it seriously." He lied, and tried to express himself with as few words as possible, because more the words, more the chances to break down, and be a weak man.

"Perfect then. Be present at the station tomorrow."

"Definitely sir."

The call was disconnected. Gregor placed the phone beside him, staring at the ceiling as if he'd just seen a ghost—a huge lizard with hungry eyes. Sweat dripped down his face. He barely slept, watching the ghost crawl from the ceiling to the walls, inching closer to his bed. Eventually, sleep overtook him, and he woke from the dream of the caterpillar.

CHAPTER SEVEN

"The police officer has asked me to be present at the station in the morning," Gregor tells his mother. "He called me at around one last night."

"But, what about your work? You've to be early today."

"I don't think it'll be possible. It's the case of a man's death."

"They found his body?" His mother asks.

Gregor nods. "That's why they're asking me to be present. I'm the only witness."

"So, what are you going to tell your boss?"

"I don't know. I can't tell him about this incident. He's already furious about me. Now he will label me as a murderer."

His mother sighs and shakes her head. "Tell him that your mother is not well, and you need to take her to the hospital."

"Yesterday I wasn't well, today my mother isn't well. No, it's not going to work, mother. He won't believe this."

"Ok, then I'll call him and tell him that you're having another seizure, and that you're going to meet the doctor."

Gregor looks at his mother for sometime and looks back at the food in front of him. "I think I should leave this job, rather than acting like a criminal every day." Gregor smiles.

"Don't even think about it, Gregor," his mother says, relaxing herself on the chair. "It's paying you quite well, and it's not just about you, but our family needs this job. Don't you see how our lives are getting better?"

Gregor nods, and looks at his mother who is smiling at him. He returns the smile.

"Give your phone, I'll tell him the lie. When people won't allow us to breathe, we will have no chance but to lie. Because we can't live without it."

"But, I don't want to lie," Gregor says this as his phone starts to ring on the table. Gregor always keeps his phone nearby as he eats. It is his boss. Gregor is confused as to why he is calling at this time, since Gregor isn't late today.

Gregor's mom takes the call, determined.

"Hello, sir... Yeah, I'm his mother... Actually no, he is not well even today. He is having a seizure... Yeah, yesterday I had asked him to go meet the doctor, but he couldn't, since he could only leave late... Yeah... Really? ... Ok sir, I will tell him... Thank you so much for understanding." Gregor's mother cut the call. "Your boss is surprisingly in a good mood today. He asked about your well-being, and when I told him that you are not well, he asked me to tell you to take the day off and go meet a doctor. Your boss is actually a good man, unlike what you tell me about him."

"He is not a good man, he is just having a good day."

"Still, I didn't expect this, you know."

Gregor nods. "But it's good that I got the day off," Gregor says. He takes his time eating breakfast, as the last meal he had was the little bit of lunch he ate yesterday afternoon. Now, without the worry of being late, Gregor asks his mother for more food, and she brings him as much as he needs.

Today, before leaving his home, Gregor doesn't forget to smile at his mother. He tells his father that he is leaving and his father asks, "Do you want me to come with you to the police station?"

"No, father. I think I can do it alone," he says.

CHAPTER EIGHT

Gregor gets into the train and finds himself sitting in a different seat than usual. Away from home, he feels like a mask has been removed from his face without his consent. At home, the people cared about him and looked him in the eye, so the mask was necessary. But here, among strangers who don't care to look at him twice, the mask falls away on its own. He feels as if he's moving through a vacuum, being drawn into an inevitable black hole. His face carries the same practiced stoic expression that he had even when he watched the man jump from the train.

Gregor raises his hand and touches the end of the antenna he can now clearly see falling in front of his face.

"My face," he whispers to himself, "is the face of death."

Hearing this, the man sitting next to him turns to look at him for a fraction of second, and in the next fraction of second, he doesn't care.

"Did you know? A guy jumped from this train, and got himself killed." There are two elderly women sitting opposite him. They have been talking to each other since they boarded the train with them, but Gregor notices them only when one of them mentions yesterday's incident.

"When?" The other woman asks.

"Just last night."

"What was the reason?"

"It is not yet known. He is the son of..." The woman begins recounting the entire genealogy of the dead man. Despite her efforts, the other woman still doesn't seem to recognize who the deceased or his relatives are. Gregor strains to hear their conversation, but they're speaking softly. The noise of the train drowns out most of their words, leaving Gregor with only fragmented bits of information—nothing useful.

"How old was he?" The other woman asks.

"He was just twenty-five. And I think the reason was money. Or maybe some love failure. You know, he was never really at home. Always travelling, saying there's one music program or the other. These artists... God knows what they are upto."

Talking bad about dead people is equal to blasphemy. Gregor doesn't know why such a thought crossed his mind, but he does not ponder much on it.

What was the reason? The woman's question revisits his mind. Only Gregor knows what the reason is, and like in most cases of suicide, it's almost impossible to explain.

CHAPTER NINE

While narrating the entire incident to the police, Gregor accidentally lets something slip. "I think he jumped when he saw my insect head," he says, the words tumbling out before he can stop them.

"Insect head?" The police officer pauses, staring at Gregor. His pen hovers above the paper, momentarily frozen.

"Yeah, my head looks like that of an insect, right?" Gregor replies, almost as if it's the most natural thing in the world.

The officer's eyes narrow. "Do you think your face has anything to do with this death?"

Gregor hesitates, feeling the weight of the officer's gaze. "Just a random thought," he mutters, regretting his slip.

The officer leans in, his voice low and stern. "Gregor, let me tell you something clearly. If your intention is to mislead the police with some stupid information, I'll call this a murder and name you as the first accused."

Gregor shakes his head, panic rising in his chest. "That is not my intention, sir," he insists, his voice trembling.

The officer doesn't respond immediately. Instead, he watches Gregor carefully, his mind racing. As he resumes writing, unwanted images start flashing through his mind. In his imagination, he sees Gregor standing by the train door with the now-dead man. The dead man turns to look at Gregor, and his face contorts with terror as he sees something monstrous—a face twisted in horror, like a grotesque mask from a classical art form the officer vaguely remembers from his childhood. The dead man jumps from the train, not out of despair, but out of sheer horror. The officer can't shake the possibility that Gregor had put a mask on, trying to deliberately scare the man, perhaps even intending to kill him.

But the officer pushes these thoughts aside, deciding not to press further on the "insect head" comment and he carries on with preparing the statement.

CHAPTER TEN

Gregor stands in the bathroom, staring into the mirror, his eyes tracing the unsettling contours of his face. The insect head, the distorted features. All that remains is a barrage of questions, each one without an answer. No matter how hard things got, he would tease his sister with silly insults, joke around, and do whatever it took to make her laugh. But today is different. Today, he can't even bear to look at her. Whenever she tries to approach him, he feels like crying, so he avoids her, shuts himself off, and spends the rest of the day in his room. He closes the windows, draws the curtains, shuts the door, and lays silently in his bed in darkness. Whenever he tries to look at the phone, he sees the antennas obstructing his vision. So he keeps the phone on the side and closes his eyes. Gregor's sister tries to open the room, and check on Gregor. But Gregor shouts at her, saying "Get off my room. Let me be alone for sometime!" Some time later, Gregor finds himself crying. How divine are tears. How lucky are those who can cry.

The Musician's funeral is at 5 in the evening, and Gregor reaches there on time. His suicide was celebrated that day in the social media, and as a result, there is a big crowd in front of his house, waiting for their chance to see him for the final time.

Gregor stands amid the crowd, looking at the people surrounding him. Most people only have curiosity in their faces, and the sheer happiness of not being the person everyone is here for, the sheer happiness of being alive. It will be a lie to say that Gregor does not feel that way.

As he walks forward, wading through the crowd, he sees a big white screen set up outside the house, where the videos of songs sung by the dead man are projected; his once vibrant voice comes out hauntingly through the speakers on either side of the white screen. Gregor also sees the very video he was watching last night seconds before he met the musician for the first time.

Gregor walks through the night road, and feels that the night has become strangely comforting to him. Maybe it is not essentially the "night", it is the "darkness" that came along with it. Gregor avoids the streetlights, and other lit corners of the road, and finds himself in that corner of the road where there is no light. He sits in front of a closed shop and remembers that this was exactly the spot where he had seen the teenagers the other night.

"Is that you?" Says a voice from behind. Gregor's eyes have by then gotten accustomed to the darkness. He sees the figure standing on the entrance to another shop. Gregor stands up and looks back at him. Gregor doesn't recognise him, but he thinks that it can be one of the teenagers he has met that night.

"I don't know what you mean," Gregor says. "But can I ask a favour?"

"What is it?"

"Look at my face, and tell me what you see."

The figure pulls out a mobile phone, flicks on the flashlight, and starts walking toward Gregor. As the light shines on him, Gregor can finally see the figure clearly. He appears to be a teenager, though Gregor cannot be certain if it is one of those he had encountered before. The man's eyes lock onto Gregor's face, and Gregor watches as his expression shifts from curiosity to sheer horror. The teenager drops his phone in shock, the device landing face down on the pavement, and then he turns and bolts into the darkness, sprinting down the road, illuminated by the streetlights as he flees. Gregor stands there, frozen, as the flashlight from the fallen phone casts a harsh light on his face. But when he glances down to where the light should be coming from, there's nothing—no beam, no phone. Confused, he looks back up, expecting to see the figure still running, but the street ahead is empty. The man may have vanished into the night, but the question remains: where is the phone?

"Gregor, what the hell are you trying to do?" Gregor's mother asks, opening the door to his bedroom. Gregor does not say anything. He just hides himself further into his bed. "You didn't eat anything last night, nothing in the afternoon, and now you're going to skip your dinner too? Food is a blessing and you are not supposed to take it for granted. What the hell has gotten into you?"

"I am not feeling hungry. Why don't you just close the door, and leave me alone? I want some time for myself. Nothing has gotten into me. I am alright."

"You're definitely destroying yourself over a dead man. Over a man you just talked to for barely an hour." Gregor's mother has started crying and he is starting to feel irritated.

"Mother please let me be."

After some time, Gregor gets up from the bed, and comes to the dining table. His mother serves him food. Gregor lifts his face slightly, so that the antennas will not brush against the food. He doesn't notice that all the eyes of his family are fixed on him, watching every move he makes. Although he isn't feeling hungry his stomach is empty and his body automatically gets him to eat the food, as much as his body needs, by taking enough time.

His mother reaches out and gently places her hand on his. "You can't do this to yourself. Even I've been upset over dead people, but those were people who were so close to us. That guy is nobody to you. We all need you to be alright and strong." His mother presses his hands.

Gregor nods. "Don't worry about me. I am alright. It's just that I'm overreacting over the death of a man I don't even know much about. I'll be alright by tomorrow, when I wake up."

His father—who had mostly been a silent but authoritative presence in his life—sits at the table, watching him intently. His father's gaze is heavy with worry, his eyes fixed on Gregor, studying every movement, every flicker of emotion. Gregor can feel the weight of his father's stare, but he keeps his own eyes cast down, avoiding any direct contact. He looks at his family, but only at their chests, never meeting their eyes.

"Gregor," his father says. "Do you think you want to see someone? As in some mental health experts or counselors, or a psychologist, maybe?"

"Our son is not crazy," his mother interjects, and everyone looks at her for a second.

"No father. I feel perfectly fine." Gregor smiles, without looking up.

"Have you gone blind?" His father raises his voice. "Can't you see me sitting right in front of you? Why aren't you looking at my face?"

Gregor doesn't say anything. His mother and sister look at him with eyes that betray concern. Gregor stops eating and gets up from his chair.

"Gregor, why are you avoiding my question?" His father's voice raises and his mother places her hand on his shoulder.

"Let him be," she says. "He did eat something, and that's a blessing. Let's not upset him now."

"You think I'm upsetting him by asking all these questions?" His voice is still raised and he also gets up and walks into his bedroom. Gregor, washes his face, and walks into his own bedroom, and slams the door shut. Gregor usually stays late at night working on something, before going to bed. But that night, his mother looks at the bottom of his bedroom door to see no light.

She comes and opens the door a bit and asks. "Do you want me to sleep with you?"

Gregor desperately wants to say yes. But he remembers that he is a big man now, who is supposed to be strong. He cannot ask his mother to sleep next to him. The words catch in his throat, tangled with emotions that have grown sharp and painful. They form a barrier, a dam that doesn't let his emotions come forth. If his mother had decided to walk into the room, and lay down next to him, Gregor knows he will not have resisted it. But instead, she quietly closes the door, returns to the seat, clears the table and makes way to her bedroom. Gregor's sister continues to stay on her chair and doesn't move a bit. No matter how closely she had lived with her brother, she is still not able to understand what is going on in his mind. She has no idea what he is going through and she wishes to help him somehow. But she can't.

Gregor rises from his bed, stumbling through the darkness, his hands groping along the walls until he reaches his desk. He finds the empty diary—a gift from his company—lying in the corner, untouched. His fingers fumble across the cluttered surface, searching until they close around a pen. Returning to his bed and opens the diary to its first blank page. Without hesitation, he begins to scribble, his hand moving feverishly across the paper, the pen scratching out words faster than his thoughts can keep up. When he finally stops, his breath catches in his throat, and the tears come. He falls asleep, exhausted, the diary slipping from his grasp.

That night in his dreams, he hears a voice that fails the clatter of the trains, and entertains him. The musician, serene and calm, faces toward the wind rushing in through the window, his lips moving effortlessly with the song that Gregor loved. Although the music makes him feel happy, it all seems disjointed. Corrupted. Gregor's eyes dart frantically around the dreamscape, searching for himself, but he can't find anything familiar. Although he is the one who sits opposite to the musician, something doesn't feel right. Panic tightens his chest, as he looks down at his own body. His once-flesh arms have sprouted into spindly, chitinuous limbs, his skin hardened into a slick, armoured carapace.

He is no longer a human.

The musician's voice wavers as he senses something amiss. He slowly turns to face Gregor. His eyes widen as he takes in the metamorphosis of the man he thought was his friend. The song has a sudden halt, the guitar, out of tune, strung for one final time. He pulls himself back and tries to defend for his life, with the voice stuck in his throat, out of horror. But it is all useless. Instead of mercy, a primal hunger overwhelms Gregor. Without warning, he lunges at the musician, his new legs propelling him forward with terrifying speed. The musician screams, but the sound is quickly drowned out by the sickening crunch of flesh and bones.

His mandibles tear into the musicians throat, painting the train car in dark red. The taste is vile, yet Gregor feels a strange sense of satisfaction as he consumes the musician's innards. He then pulls himself back, turning the musician's body into a mangled, unrecognisable husk.

Gregor wakes up with a start, sweating all over. The first face he sees upon waking up, is that of his sister. She sits on Gregor's chair, going through the diary, which Gregor wrote last night. Those are written in the darkness, so the words do not have any order, and some words were written on top of the other, making it almost impossible to read.

"Who asked you to read my diary?" Gregor shouts and his voice stuns her. She looks at him. Gregor isn't looking at her face, instead he is looking at the diary. It is as if Gregor has taken a resolution to avoid eye contact with everyone.

"Did you write this last night?"

Gregor doesn't reply.

"You used to write like this when you were really young. Back then, I was able to read what you have written. But now I understand literally nothing. What is this?"

"Those are just my thoughts. Nothing worthwhile."

"Nothing worthwhile? Your thoughts matter to me. It matters to our mother... father... why are you not saying anything?"

"You will not understand."

Gregor snatches the diary from her, and looks at it. At first it looks like the scribblings of a madman, that means nothing. But on close examination, Gregor is able to understand what was in his mind, while scribbling those words. He finds words and the sentences, and the meaning it carries.

"Back then, you used to write stories," his sister begins. "Stories about an insect who attends school. It always used to sit alone without attempting to make friends, because it is different from everyone else, and no one will be ready to accept it and become friends. You wrote about its loneliness, about its sorrows. But now, when I read this diary, I found a word which looked exactly like insect. More than once."

Gregor looks down. He feels as if he is caught. He wonders what to tell her, how to convince her that he is alright and nothing is what she thinks it is. He wonders how to avoid the situation, and continue with his normal life.

"You're just imagining things," Gregor says, finally. "It's true that I used to write such stories back then. But I stopped writing it a long time ago. I don't know. His death has affected me more than it should have. So, last night, I wanted to write my thoughts down to get some clarity. And here you're imagining different things."

"You turned the light off. Nobody writes in pitch darkness, unless they want to write things that nobody else should be reading."

"I couldn't stand the light. Maybe it's the headache, and I wanted to write, no matter what. That's how this happened." Gregor gets up, and keeps the diary in its place on the table, and turns to look at her, without having an eye contact with her. "Also, stop invading my space, and looking into my belongings without my permission. I wouldn't like that. Now get out."

She gets up and walks out of the room, in anger. Gregor takes his watch from the table, and looks at the time. He is getting late.

Gregor has started ignoring his own face in the mirror. He brushes his teeth looking at the wall, and bathes himself, and whenever he accidentally catches a glimpse of his own face, he suddenly turns his head away. He eats breakfast just to make his mother happy and rushes out of the house, carefully avoiding her face and not betraying a smile.

Gregor has also stopped observing the people around him, as he travels and walks on the street. Even when others come near to talk, Gregor efficiently concludes the conversation in just two exchanges, or he simply ignores them. When he is on the train, he plugs in his earphones and listens to some sad songs that strangely comfort him and make him feel better. He, as usual, tries to perfect himself in the art of not being affected by anyone, even when he is surrounded by people. The last time he showed some interest in someone, it damaged him beyond repair.

On a very normal day without any unprecedented happenings, Gregor is always the first person to reach the office. He comes alone, sits at his table and starts working without actually waiting for anyone else. Today is a similar day. Gregor arrives early and starts working as usual. He has a bunch of work pending, owing to the leave that his boss had allowed him yesterday. His boss, who is otherwise early, is the last person to arrive today, and the first thing he does upon arrival is calling Gregor into his room.

"So, tell me, how did the meeting with the doctor go?" The boss says. He is relaxing on his chair, falling back, with one leg over the other. He is reclined on the chair, as if waiting for someone to come in and give him a massage. He closes his eyes and his head falls behind. Gregor thinks that this man is going to sleep. Gregor looks at his hairless head, and the potbelly which is tucked into his pants and is held tightly by a brown belt. Gregor on the other hand, sits straight on his chair, with his palms closed and resting on the table that separates them. Gregor for a moment, remembers the day he had been in this room for the first time, for the final stage of his interview. That day, Gregor was not sitting straight, he was rather reclining in a more relaxed and confident manner, looking at the boss in his eyes, and answering questions impressively. That day, his boss was leaning towards Gregor, clearly attracted to his talents and confidence, wanting to ask him questions, and listen to his replies. It was more like a first date, where both are clearly interested in each other. That day, he felt that he was slightly superior to his boss, although that was the only day he had felt that way. When Gregor was selected for the post, he accepted the offer mainly because of how pleasant he had felt with the boss, and something in his mind kept on telling him that he was never going to meet a better boss again.

Gregor is about to give an answer to the question asked to him, when his boss cuts him short. "Ahh. That monkey didn't come to pick me up in the morning," the boss said, mentioning his personal assistant, who drives his car. "He instead sent an utter fool. That guy took me all over the city, before dropping me here. Doesn't know left and right. An incompetent fool. I was asleep, and when I woke up I realised that I was getting late. Monkey deserves a good flogging tomorrow. Don't you think so? You know people have to be responsible for their job, and give importance to it over everything, because it provides them with money to sustain. Without money, you're nothing but a dead mosquito stuck on the wall. What do you think about people who refuse to show up to work? Without them, how is the company supposed to run? Do you think, when an employee is absent, our company can perform at its best?"

Gregor shakes his head.

"Gregor, say something. This is not a monologue. I'm trying to have a conversation with you."

"I don't think the company can perform at its best sir. When an employee is absent."

"Exactly! Look at the example of our monkey. Because of his absence, I lost an hour, which is precious for our company. What a coincidence, you were also absent yesterday, and yes, it has affected our company too. Don't you think so?"

"Yes sir."

"Then, why do you avoid work, stating stupid reasons?"

Gregor feels as if all words have left his body. He fumbles his mind for some to cover for himself. But he does not know what to say. He looks at the boss in his eyes, as if he is being asked by a policeman Gregor, you killed the man, right? Gregor is unaccustomed to lies. Gregor can't tell a lie by looking at the face of a man. Gregor feels cornered, as if on a battlefield. He looks at the empty quiver and the only option left with him is to surrender. To put both his palms behind his neck and accept defeat.

"Sir... I..."

"You've no excuse, right?" The boss says. He is still in his resting position. He looks at Gregor with a smile, such a smile that someone looking at the scene from outside would mistake it for a friendly one. Gregor turns to the wall, to see a bug relaxing over there, and his heart skips a beat.

"As I have already told you, I wasn't well these days, and yesterday I went to see the doctor," Gregor starts.

"Ah! A bug! The janitor gets paid for nothing! Gregor, why is there a bug in my room?" The boss says, suddenly getting out of his reclining posture, and sitting in his usual hunching position, looking at the bug on the left wall.

Gregor shakes his head, without knowing how to respond to that. Is this man kidding?

"Although it's the janitor's fault, everyone in the office is equally responsible for this." The boss said, pointing at the bug. "It shows the hygiene of each one of you."

Gregor sits frozen to his seat, and he feels as if his head had gotten stuck on top of his neck. He wishes that his boss will leave him alone; that this creepy interrogation will end soon, and he can go back to his table.

"Gregor, do you really want this job?"

"Yes. I do, sir."

"But you're behaving as if I'm the one who is benefitting from your job. Gregor, when I say that I don't like something, you need to find ways to solve that issue. For instance, now I expressed my discomfort on seeing a bug in my room, and you're simply sitting in front of me, and listening to me as if I'm telling some fucking fairy tale."

"I'm sorry, sir." Gregor looks at his boss, without really understanding what he meant.

The boss slaps at his forehead. "This fucking moron," he whispers, but loud enough for Gregor to hear. "Gregor, please don't make me furious. You will not like it."

Gregor continues to look at him with a blank face. "I'm sorry, sir."

"Boy, I'm not sitting here to listen to your sorry's. Why don't you just get up and do something to get rid of that insect?" The boss says. His expression calms down in an instant. He puts on his glasses and opens his laptop, as if Gregor has left the room, and now he can return to his work. But Gregor is still sitting in front of him, like an invisible presence, unsure of what to do.

Gregor rises himself up from the chair. He reaches to his right foot and removes the shoe. He moved slowly and silently, caring to make no noise with the shoe on his other foot. He reaches the wall and he can now see the bug closely. He looks at its face and thinks that it looks similar to his own. For a moment, a thought crosses his mind that he is going to kill himself. But the sanest part of his brain keeps on telling him that that is not the case. He shakes these thoughts off his mind. He brings the shoe closer to the bug, so that its tip is almost touching it. He slaps the bug with one fatal blow, and the insect falls down injured. He sees the bug laying on its back, struggling to move, with its legs moving frantically as if in a mania. It reminds Gregor of himself on the day before yesterday, when he woke up and couldn't get himself off from the body of a bug.

Gregor looks at the boss. He is still focused on his work, but when Gregor is about to leave the room, the boss calls his name. "Where the fuck are you leaving? First of all, clear the insect from the floor, and clean the wall, I can still see the stain on it." Gregor does not say anything in return, but he stares at the boss. Sometimes, when words don't come out of the mind, it gets metamorphosed into facial expressions, and these facial expressions betray nature. The boss looks down. "Or else, leave it. I'll tell my assistant to do that. You come here and be seated. We haven't finished talking, right?"

Gregor obeys.

"Look at your eyes! Haven't you been sleeping well lately?"

"I have no issues with sleep, sir. I've been sleeping quite well recently."

"I don't believe that. I do believe that something is bothering you," the boss says smiling, like a friend or a trained counselor.

Gregor shakes his head.

"Gregor, tell me honestly. Have you been involved with the police in any way?"

"No, sir," Gregor's facial features suddenly change. His eyes widen and his skin tightens.

"But that is not what I've heard."

The boss isn't looking at Gregor, but Gregor looks only at him, and he looks for any change in his face, and tries to predict what he is going to say next.

"Did you kill someone?" He asks, and just then, the bug which was on the floor, flis and lands on the table that separates them. "Fuck it Gregor! Didn't you kill this little piece of shit?" The boss panics. He gets a giant book that comes handy, and lands it on the bug with full might. The sound is so loud and unexpected that Gregor shuts his ears, and closes his eyes.

The boss takes the book off the bug. Gregor sees the insect crushed, and its body parts seperated. One of its legs is still moving, like the only part of its tiny body that proves that it is not completely dead.

"Now that's how you kill an insect." The boss says. Gregor has his hands covering his forehead, and he looks before him as if he has just witnessed a murder. "What the fuck is wrong with you? Why are you behaving strangely?"

Gregor covers his mouth with a hand, and his body shakes as if he is having a terrible fever.

"Gregor," the boss stands up, and reaches out to his shoulder.

"Sir, I'm... okay," he stammers, although his body is now shaking violently. He tries to get up from the chair, but he falls down. He is now on his knees and he bends over, his face touching the floor. His colleagues have arrived at the door, and they watch it as if it is a spectacle. None of them comes over to help or support him. Gregor has always been a self-indulgent, selfish man, and now it is reciprocated back to him.

The boss watches all this with sudden surprise. He looks back and forth at Gregor, and the other employees who had arrived by the door.

Gregor stays like that for five long minutes, then he tries to get up, holding onto the chair. He acts as if he has lost his balance. His face is downcasted, and when he looks up at the boss, the boss is surprised to see his bloodshot eyes and pale face. Gregor tries to stand upright, by balancing his body on the chair. He looks at the employees as if in embarrassment and suddenly turns away from them, as if he is shy.

"Sir, may I use the toilet."

The boss nods and holds his hands in the direction of the door. The employees make way for him, as he walks out of the cabin.

"Such a clown!" The boss says to the employees, after Gregor has moved away, groping through chairs and desks, to the bathroom.

Gregor turns the tap on, and stands in front of the mirror, looking back at the insect head of a person he doesn't know. He walks to a corner of the bathroom, and sits down, with his head buried in between his knees. He gets up, opens the door and walks back to his boss's cabin. His colleagues had by then gotten back to their respective tables.

Gregor asks his permission to get in, and the boss allows.

"Will you try to kill me again?" The boss asks, with a mocking smile.

Gregor shakes his head. "Sir, I wasn't trying to harm you in any way."

"Oh, I wish that wasn't the case," the boss says. "You know what was the thought that crossed my head when I saw you like that?"

Gregor shakes his head.

"That there is no difference between you and this insect," the boss says and laughs as if he is trying to make a joke. "Gregor, I don't think I've a good sense of humour, but that was good, and it's an insult that you didn't laugh."

"Sir, trust me, that wasn't a good joke," Gregor says, without any change in expression. He looks down at the insect that is still resting on the table. "Sir, the insect, let me clear it."

"Use this paper," the boss gets a fresh piece of paper from the side table and passes it over to Gregor. Gregor raises the insect with its antenna, his hand still shaking slightly, and places the insect on the piece of paper, and folds it. He gets up and throws the folded paper in the waste bin. He returns to his chair, and looks back at the boss with a stern glance.

"Gregor, is it just me, or do you actually look like an insect?"

"It's not just you, sir. My school friends used to think the same, and now I'm starting to realise that it is true."

The boss laughs for quite a long time, and he finds it difficult to stop.

"I bet it's by seeing your insect figure that the guy jumped off his train, right?" The boss continues laughing.

Gregor looks at his boss with anxiety sending heat waves throughout his body.

"But we can't completely rule out the fact that you pushed that man off the train. If someone says that you killed the man, I would believe it, because you are capable of doing it."

Gregor has his face downcasted. He is wondering what to say as a reply.

"Boy, next time be very careful when hiding things from me. Oh no, but I do really doubt if there is a next time, you know? Maybe, there isn't." The boss laughs, and Gregor has never seen him laugh so much. "Gregor, do you realise how many reasons I have to fire you?"

"Sir, I promise I'm not involved in the case, in any way. I'm only a witness, and the police have almost proved my innocence."

"I'm almost not a murderer," the boss laughs, and Gregor wants to get up and strangle him until he dies. "Gregor, do you realise that you aren't making any sense?"

Gregor shakes his head helplessly. He wants to cry. But there is no way he can let the tears pass through his eyes and make himself look weak.

"Gregor, there are records to prove that you've been stealing money from the company," the boss says. Gregor tries to interrupt, but the boss signals him to hold the thought and let him continue. "You're making up excuses to avoid work and arrive late, you're getting involved in police cases, and right now you tried to harm me with your delirium. Maybe, I'm sorry to say this, Gregor, maybe it's better if you give in your resignation. It's better than getting fired."

Gregor is silent. He looks at the boss, and at the table where the bug had been. He then gets up from the chair. "Ok, sir. I'm leaving."

"You can talk to the HR about the formalities. Then you can send me a resignation email directly."

Gregor, as he walks out of the office, wonders whether he should go back in and tell his boss about how much he needed this job, and make him rethink his decision. The only face that crosses his mind is that of his mother. He remembers what she had told him yesterday morning. He wonders how he will share this news with her. Gregor thinks about the guy who had jumped out of the train in front of his eyes. Gregor stops on his way back to the office, when that thought crosses his mind. He stands as if someone had suddenly pressed a pause button on him. He stands in the middle of all of his co-workers who stop their work to observe him. Gregor stands like a grim reaper, clothed in black overalls, his oversized black shirt gone out of the tucked in position. He shrinks inside his big pants, and it looks as if he is covered using black clothes. He stands there looking down, without having the energy to move forward. All his co-workers are watching him. His boss is also on his feet, with his eyes on him, through the open window. Nobody comes near him and asks if he is alright. Gregor had never wanted anyone to ask him that, and even at this moment, he does not want anyone to come closer to him, and put their hand on his shoulder. He does not want to invite anyone's attention to himself. But at this moment, Gregor feels like it is incorrect to take a step forward.

Gregor hears his name being called from behind. He turns back to see his boss standing there, with his hands spread as if asking him what's wrong.

"Are you trying to put on a show?" The boss asks.

Gregor shakes his head. His face is downcasted, and he is watching the firm feet of his boss in shiny leather shoes.

"The corporate world is unforgiving. It's often ungrateful too. People rarely get a second chance here. There's no point in whining and getting depressed over it," the boss says. "But, I'm ready to give you another chance to prove yourself, and consider this the last chance you'll ever get in your entire lifetime. Understood?" Gregor nods, his head still hanging low. "Get back to your workspace, now." The boss says and walks back to his cabin. Gregor raises his head and watches him go. Gregor suddenly has two choices before him. He can either go to the HR room and talk about his resignation, or walk to his own workplace and continue with his work. He places a step towards the HR rooms, then an image of his mother's face flashes through his mind. He took the step back, and turned towards his workspace instead. Gregor has never thought about running away from the job he had at hand, because he knows that no matter where he is at, there will be some aspect that he will like, and some aspect he will not. He had never considered resignation until today; until what had happened today in the boss's cabin.

Gregor walks towards his chair. He is starting to feel nauseous like every other day, and today it seems more intense than ever. He takes the tablet he always carried with him in his bag, and takes one along with water. He then massages the sides of his head. He sits straight, takes a deep breath, and takes in the brightness of the monitor in front of him. He makes a mental reminder to buy a pair of glasses that would aid his eyes from the strong light. From that moment, till the end of the workday, Gregor, his boss and his colleagues, behaves as if nothing had happened in the morning, as if the corporate is not just unforgiving and ungrateful, but also unreal.

CHAPTER ELEVEN

"Look at my hand," she says.

Gregor breaks eye contact with her, and remembers that she has a body, not just a face. He finds it difficult to look away from her eyes as if they had a magnetic force that kept him hooked. He looks down, and sees her insect hand. She moves it to make Gregor believe that it is all true.

"See? That's why I can see your insect body and your insect face. I am not afraid of it." She says in her melodious tone. "Tell me more about your interest in wood sculpting."

Gregor studies her full cheeks that widen even more when she smiles, and the freckles on her nose, and beneath her eyes. She wears a blue frock with white powder design that makes it look like a night sky with stars.

The train goes faster as usual, and her hair travels along with it. She struggles to put her loose hair strands in place. Her lips seem to have a permanent smile stuck on them. Maybe it is always there, or it is there only for Gregor, because that smile is there from the moment he has seen her, and it has never once faded, for even a second.

"Your smile," Gregor says.

"What?" She says.

"No, I think I heard the question wrong. Can you ask it again?"

"Tell me about your interest in wood sculpting. Because, I am also interested in it."

"No way!" Gregor says with a laugh. "I thought it was an odd hobby only I had."

"I don't think anyone has an original hobby, Gregor. We all share it. We all share experiences, hobbies, and habits."

"Yeah. I know it now," Gregor says. "Just that I have never met anyone with the same hobby as mine. You know I have even been into some dating apps, trying to find someone like me. But it's impossible."

She nods with her usual laugh. "I know."

Gregor looks at her and takes the moment in for some time. Then he breaks her eye contact.

"It's actually a childhood hobby, to be honest, because I don't get the time or even the energy to pursue that hobby now," Gregor says. "You know, as a child, my ambition was to be a carpenter. But later it changed to an office worker."

"A big downgrade. A big downgrade," she says, her eyes widened. Her face is now closer to him. But she then falls back into her seat, and looks outside the window.

"Yeah. It was a big upgrade to me back then. But now I know it wasn't. What interested me was carpenting. But I almost said goodbye to it forever. Just the previous Sunday, while I was at home, I made a picture frame with wood. My sister paints well, so she gifted a picture for me on my previous birthday. I had always kept it inside a file all this while, only now got the chance to actually frame it."

She nods. "I am married by the way," she says, showing the ring in her left hand.

"Can your husband see your insect hand?" Gregor asks.

"Of course not," she says. "As I said, there are some people in this world, with experiences similar to us. Only such people can see us, and understand us."

Gregor nods. "Like you and me."

"Exactly, Gregor," she says. "Where were you all these days?"

"Hidden in the darkness." Gregor says and laughs.

"I've been in the dark, too. Just now got a chance to breathe," she says, and looks at Gregor in a way that makes Gregor speechless. "Insects like us always stay in the dark."

Gregor keeps on looking at her. He tries, but he cannot look away. She has been looking at him too. If it were anyone else, Gregor would have already felt discomfort and had looked away.

"When I tell my husband that my left hand is like that of an insect, he just doesn't believe me. He used to listen to me at first. Now, he says that I am crazy."

"You atleast have someone to share it with. I don't."

"You have your sister, who is so thoughtful."

Gregor shakes his head. "No, she'll not be interested in all this."

"Alright. Now you have someone to share it with, right?"

"Yeah. I must say, it feels good. It's as if a burden has been taken away from me."

She nods, with the same smile she had on her face when they saw for the first time.

"I like your face, you know," he says.

"But, I'm too scared to look at it."

"And I can't stop looking at it."

"You said you like wood sculpting too," Gregor says, changing the topic.

"Yes. But it's the same as you. Got drowned in the mundane. Marriages, work and everything," she says and looks outside the train window. She looks at the world that is going behind her. "I liked to make toys, you know. Everyone used to love what I did. After I had my first child, I tried to sculpt something for her. But it didn't work. I started working on it and I ended up hating myself. I have not tried to do anything for the past six years."

Gregor nods. "Not being able to do something that you've once loved doing. What is more hurtful than that?"

The smile is still on her face, and Gregor loves looking at it, when she isn't facing him.

"Don't you think I'm scary?" Gregor says pointing at his face.

She looks at him, sizing him up. She shakes her head in response. "Believe me, you aren't. Look how I'm talking to you. Look how happy I am. The question is totally out of place. Or, you think this way. What do you think about my left hand? Isn't it scary too?"

Gregor shakes his head. "It's not. In fact, I feel like I want to hold it."

She looks at him with a smile, which is the same, but has started to carry different meanings. Her smile is an art and she is an artist. Everyone looks at the artwork and interprets it in different ways. "Hold it, then." She extends her insect hand towards him.

He reaches his hands to touch it. But when he almost touches it, she pulls it back.

"What do you think will happen after you hold my hand?"

Gregor shakes his head, signaling that he does not know.

She again pulls her hand before him. He tries to touch it, but he can't. All he can feel is thin air.

"Why can't I touch it?"

She continues to smile.

"Why?"

She takes her hand back.

"I think I'll feel the same, if I try to touch your face," she says.

"Touch it, then."

"No, I don't want to be disappointed," she says.

"Please try it."

She shakes her head and falls back on her seat. The smile vanishes from her face, as she sits like that, looking outside the window.

"You know, it'll be a great disappointment if we won't be able to hold hands and kiss."

Gregor is confused. He touches his head as he continues to think.

"I'll hold your right hand."

"Look at my right hand," she says.

He turns to see that the woman sitting in front of him doesn't have a right hand.

"An accident. It was after this that I started getting visions of my insect hand," she says, raising her left hand a bit. Gregor looks at it, and is lost in thought. "Do you think our visions are just games that our mind plays or are we given a blessing to see what others can't?"

She looks at him, and he shakes his head. "I would like to think it is a blessing. Because, if it is a mind game, then it means that something is wrong with my mind."

She nods. "My husband even took me to a therapist. But it didn't work. I stopped it without telling him, and he doesn't care. It's mostly due to our lifestyle, I guess. If we need an escape, we need to make conscious decisions, alter our lifestyle, but even then, nothing is sure." She looks at Gregor and he is looking at her now. "When did you start seeing your insect head?"

"Actually it's not just my head. I used to see that I had turned into an insect, like a total metamorphosis. But, mostly it's just my head. Sometimes I even forget how I looked, then I check some of my photos on my phone. It's difficult," he says. "Why is the train taking longer than usual?"

"Am I boring you?"

"No, you aren't."

"So, answer me. I think you're too good at dodging questions."

"I don't like to get too personal." Gregor laughs.

"It's alright. I'm not forcing you."

"It's nothing important," Gregor says and sits straight. He looks at her, and she is looking back at him, encouraging. "I was born in a quiet, secluded area. My childhood was too boring to say the least. No friends to play with, and even in school, I was bullied and was probably the last person you would notice. I used to hide myself from everyone. My friends used to call me an insect, telling me that I looked like one. Moreover, my parents used to beat me and shout at me, for literally anything I did. Anything, no matter how small it is. So one night, my father beat me like a dog. I went to sleep sobbing. I had difficulty sleeping, but I slept some time before dawn.

"It was that morning that I started getting visions. My parents thought that I was having seizures. Since then, they've been treating me nicely. They've never beat me, or even raised their voice at me after that. They allowed me to be with my friends, and also informed my tutors about my health issues and asked them to be nice to me. They also took me to the doctor and treated me. I got better. I still got bullied. But, what do the bullies know? They're also little children like me trying to comprehend the world. But after that, I stopped having seizures and life was going good. And now, those visions have returned, stronger than ever. I can't call it demons. Maybe they're bugs, who've come to haunt me from the past."

"I've learnt to love my demons, or my bugs as you say. I love my insect hand, more than any other part of mine."

"I hate it, and I'm too scared. I don't even have the confidence to share it with anyone."

"Gregor, you just shared it with me."

"Because I knew that nobody in this world would understand me better than you."

"There might be many people who are just like us, and some of them would understand you better than me; you'd be surprised. But, it is too difficult to find them. Especially for people like us, who hide in the darkness." She laughed. "You want my number?"

"Of course."

She shares her number. He types it in his phone, and calls her. Her phone rings on her lap. She looks down.

"Today is a Friday, right?" She asks.

"Is it?"

"Yeah. Friday evenings are the best, isn't it?"

Gregor checks his phone. "No! Oh God! Today's a Monday! I can't be late!" He says.

"What?"

"I don't know."

Gregor feels as if the whole world has blacked out, and only he remains as if in a spotlight. The woman who had been sitting in front of him has disappeared. The darkness seems solid. It tries to bind him, as if to suffocate him. The darkness is a human now. It has its hand on Gregor's throat. The grip tightens and it feels as if he would pass out any moment.

Green Apples

CHAPTER TWELVE

Gregor wakes up with a start to the loud sound of his bed crashing. He feels himself sliding off the bed, almost hitting the floor. That's when he opens his eyes and tries to pull himself back up. He realizes it was all just a dream. *Why do we hear voices that never exist?*

When Gregor wakes, he feels as if he's been asleep for four days straight. It takes him over a minute to fully return to reality. Although he remembers the essence of the dream, the details are already slipping away. He sits on the bed, trying to recall it—the woman... the conversation they were having... what she was going through... how she empathized with him... the words they shared...

He stands up and looks at the clock—he's already half an hour late. He doesn't have the energy to face the day. He wants to sink back into the comfort of the bed and return to that dream, though he knows it's nearly impossible. The image of his boss yelling at him haunts him more than the realization that the woman he was just talking to was only a figment of his imagination. What is fantasy, when reality is right there, ready to knock you down? Gregor picks up the pace, walks towards the bathroom, and shuts the door behind him.

While waiting for the train, Gregor checks the WhatsApp statuses and realizes it's his sister's birthday today. Since starting his job, there are no dates—just days. There are no birthdays, only workdays and holidays. On workdays, you work hard, and on holidays, you sleep. Gregor makes a mental note to buy his sister a gift, perhaps her favorite cake, on his way home.

"When is your birthday?" Gregor remembers asking a girl, nearly four years ago.

"December 14th," she replied.

"Really?"

"Yes. Why?"

"It's the same day as my sister's."

"It's okay, I don't mind sharing my birthday with her."

While on the train, he wishes he could forget her. The last time he saw her was at the railway station, almost a month ago. She was alone, wearing a blue kurti, her handbag slung over her shoulder, standing right in front of him. He wanted to move closer, to ask her where she had been or how she was doing. But he couldn't move an inch. Whenever she glanced in his direction, she looked right through him, as if he were invisible. That day, the train seemed to take longer than usual to arrive. Gregor felt uncomfortable, plagued by the thoughts swirling in his mind. He wanted to approach her and talk as though nothing had ever happened between them. He wanted to speak to her like an old friend—or even as a new one—to meet her again, get to know her all over again, ask her name, and become friends. But Gregor just stood there.

Most people in Gregor's life are transitory. His relationships with them are brief, and they leave him, for one reason or another. Maybe, deep down, it's what Gregor wants. He doesn't want to get too attached and break himself in the worst possible way. Though that thought lingers in the back of his mind, she was different. She was one of the few people he had wanted to talk to for years and years... But they spoke for only six months before she left him. Gregor wanted to walk up to her and ask what those six months had meant, though he already knew the answer: *they meant nothing.*

Gregor remembers the nights he spent crying over her. The night he returned home after their final conversation, he walked into the bathroom, sat on the toilet, and cried his heart out. Then there were those lonely nights that followed, when he would release the tears that had been bottled up in his mind. Wounds on the mind are the worst. Physical wounds heal with time, but what about the ones we can't see?

It's been four years now, and Gregor tries to remind himself it's long past time to stop thinking about her.

Reels: the only way out. The "harmless" way to forget. A seemingly innocent alternative to drugs. People had been waiting for something like this, and it was given to them. Pick up the phone, scroll mindlessly. Watch people make fools of themselves, laugh, and forget. Life is easier and happier that way.

Gregor watches the people around him, all fixated on their phones. Everyone, heads bent down, gazing at the world unravelling inside their palms. They don't talk to each other. Silence surrounds him. He tries to identify the insects sitting around him. The thin man in the green shirt looks like a caterpillar. That tall guy over there could be a cockroach. The woman in the red dress—maybe a ladybug. The little girl by the window, playing some random game on her mother's phone, could be a butterfly. Gregor imagines her with butterfly wings and smiles. The little girl notices him, frowns, and then returns to her screen. Gregor turns away, plugs in his earphones, and listens to some old songs. He closes his eyes, hoping to drift off and return to his dream, to meet the girl in the red dress again.

Gregor wonders why the world suddenly turns into a monochrome film whenever he steps into the office. It happens every day, but today it feels more vivid. Even though he's late, he's still the first one to arrive. As usual, he walks to his desk and begins his work. Throughout the day, he watches people trickle in. As always, he observes them not with sorrow, but with relief that they greet everyone else but him.

There's a meeting that day, as there is every day, between Gregor's marketing team and the Boss. These meetings usually happen when the Boss has no one else to gossip with. They start with project discussions but, within minutes, devolve into mindless chatter that drags on for at least two hours. Gregor sometimes wonders if the Boss arranges these meetings to teach them the value of time. As the meeting progresses and the Boss rambles about topics unrelated to work, Gregor glances at his watch, saddened by the seconds slipping away. He wishes he could reclaim that time—not to be productive, but at least to spend it on his own terms rather than wasting it on someone else's whims.

But then Gregor realizes that's all he's been doing for the past three years. Sometimes, he wonders how different his life would have been if he'd spent those years doing something he enjoyed. He might have been free, but his parents would still be living the miserable lives they once had. When he thinks about how his family and their home have improved in the last three years, he feels a sense of pride and convinces himself that what he's doing is worthwhile.

Time drags in these meetings, even when Gregor tries to focus and take an interest in the Boss's random gossip. Afterward, he feels as though he's worked overtime, completely drained and too exhausted to continue working. After that, it's just a countdown to six o'clock.

CHAPTER THIRTEEN

Gregor mostly sleeps on his way back home, listening to songs that aren't quite his taste, but soothing enough to lull him into slumber. He recently started wearing a hat outside of work, an unusual sight in his town, but useful for concealing his face. He wears it over his face while he sleeps and pulls it over his head when he walks the streets. The hat, paired with his slightly hunched posture, helps him avoid attention—though ironically, it sometimes draws more curiosity. Still, it's difficult to see his face without a closer look. As he dozes with the hat covering his face, he misses the beauty of the sun setting over the river, casting brilliant shades of red, orange, and blue over the water as the train crosses the bridge. He doesn't notice the faint glow of the full moon against a purple sky. Even in sleep, Gregor seems to make a conscious effort to shield himself, turning away from the world and from eyes that might notice him. Even when his dreams are haunted by meaningless horrors, he still manages to carry on as if everything were normal.

Back when the incident with the teenagers happened, Gregor feared walking the dark streets, always expecting an attack from the shadows. But now, he feels more at peace, as if the darkness has become a part of him. Without it, he senses he wouldn't be happy.

As he nears his house, something unusual catches his attention. The house is adorned with soft yellow lights. Though the lights aren't glaringly bright, they still make him uncomfortable, triggering an instinctive reaction to shield his eyes. Darkness had become his home, and now, in the presence of light, he feels homesick for the shadows.

"Are you Nita's brother?" a voice calls from behind. Gregor turns to see a slender young man with long hair, as if he's practicing to become a monk. A faint mustache lines his upper lip, and he smiles warmly, seemingly thrilled to meet Nita's brother, someone he's only heard about. But Gregor has no idea who this guy is.

For a moment, Gregor wants to say no and head back the way he came. He even turns to leave. But if he leaves, he has no place else to go that he can call home. Maybe his office is his second home—or is it his first? Gregor isn't sure anymore, but in any case, it isn't open at this hour.

Gregor looks up at the young man and nods. "Yes."

"Come. Everyone's waiting for you inside."

"You shouldn't have waited for me," Gregor wants to say, but he remains silent.

As Gregor steps into the house, he takes in the decorations with a sense of awe. His home has never looked like this before. A smile begins to form on his face, but it quickly fades when he remembers that he's the only earning member of his family.

As a brother, he feels he should have been the one organizing a surprise party for his sister. But instead, the party has come as a surprise to him. His parents, sister, her friends, and some relatives are gathered around a large cake, all waiting for Gregor to arrive.

"Why are you wearing a hat?" his mother asks.

Gregor realizes he had forgotten to take it off. He removes the hat, and, unbeknownst to him, several of the girls present feel their hearts skip a beat. Gregor, though unaware, is tall and striking, with thick hair that naturally draws attention. His chiseled features and serious expression give him an air of mystery. When he offers a smile to the group—a forced, obligatory smile—it nevertheless lights up the room, especially for the women. But Gregor is oblivious. To him, the smile is just a formality, a reflex when people look his way. Although he's been complimented for his looks in the past, Gregor only believes the ones who criticize him, assuming that those who praise him are just being polite or lying.

As the party begins, and his sister cuts the cake while everyone sings the usual birthday song, Gregor notices a girl among her friends. She has a radiant smile, and as she sings and claps along, her face seems to glow with a kind of beauty that makes Gregor smile—this time, a real smile. But when her eyes meet his, Gregor quickly turns his gaze away, unsure of where to look. His eyes settle on the cake. This cake doesn't look so great, he thinks, shrugging to himself.

Throughout the party, Gregor finds himself glancing at her, but she avoids looking his way, perhaps sensing his attention. The only time their eyes meet again is when she approaches to say goodbye. She smiles, and Gregor returns it—a smile that is as fake as it is bright.

The perfect day to forget someone is the day you feel the pull of new attraction. And what easier way to forget than by mindlessly scrolling through reels, designed to capture your attention and never give it back. That night, Gregor feels unusually sleepy and drifts off as he scrolls through the endless feed.

In the dream, Gregor sees their home transformed, adorned lavishly as if for a wedding. People bustle in and out, and Gregor moves among them, uncertain of his purpose or place. No one notices him, but their awe is palpable, focused entirely on the extravagant decorations that have left everyone speechless.

"I've never seen anything like this in my entire life," one guest says to another. They heap admiration upon the beauty of the house, their words overflowing with every good adjective.

Amidst the dream, Gregor finds himself talking to a man who looks exactly like his sister's friend—the one he had met outside the house that evening.

"Sir, here's the bill," the man says.

"Bill for what?" Gregor asks.

"All this," the man replies, gesturing toward the decorations around them.

"Give it to me."

The man hands him a piece of paper. Gregor looks at it, and a sinking feeling overwhelms him. Tens, hundreds, thousands... The numbers blur, impossible to count. He looks back at the man, whose wide smile reveals a row of gleaming teeth.

"Who's that person standing behind you?" Gregor asks, his voice faltering.

The man turns, searching behind him. "Where, sir?"

"By the curtains." Gregor points to the far end of the room. There, between long white curtains, silhouetted against the soft light streaming in from a window, stands a figure—a man dressed in black overalls, wearing a large hat that obscures his face. Gregor can't see the man's eyes, but somehow, he knows the man is watching him, almost studying him. His heart sinks further as he squints, trying to discern the figure's face. "Why... why does he look like me?" Gregor whispers.

Gregor jolts awake. He grabs his phone to check the time—it's almost three in the morning. The fan is spinning at full speed, yet his body is drenched in sweat. His hair is damp as he runs his fingers through it, and his breathing is ragged. December's chill should have kept him comfortable, but he feels suffocated. He stands up and walks to the sink, splashing cold water onto his hands.

The scene reminds him of another night, years ago. That night, he had also woken at three, restless and disturbed. He hadn't wanted to turn on the lights, fearing the brightness would ruin his chance of falling back asleep. Instead, he glanced into the mirror, catching sight of the faint light seeping through the curtains. That's when he saw him—a man, standing by the curtains, wearing a hat and a jacket. Gregor's instinct was to scream, but when he spun around, the space before the curtain was empty. Only darkness remained.

On another night, he saw the same man again, this time sitting on a chair near the curtain. But once more, when Gregor turned to confront him, he found nothing but an empty chair. Time and again, the man appeared in his reflection—standing or sitting, always near the curtains, always just beyond reach.

He stands at the wash and turns the light on. As he brings his hands underneath the tap, and turns the tap on, he looks at the mirror, at the curtains, whether the man is still there. But he isn't. He looks at the chairs around the dining table, and everywhere near the window, but there is no one. His eyes wander and finally stop at his own reflection. He feels the pain of a spear passing through his ribs, piercing his heart. He looks at his insect head, and when he looks down, he sees that his body has also changed. He brings his hands in front of his eyes and finds that he isn't a human anymore. He stands there, looking at the human being standing in front of him, who has completely metamorphosed into an insect. Something inside him tells that the figure he used to see standing by the curtain, was no one but him. A man with the body of an insect, with his entire body covered in a jacket, hiding his face with a hat, looking helplessly at the man he once used to be. Gregor stands there, looking at his own face, not aware of what he may do. He remembers the life he used to live as a normal being, who only had problems outside of himself. Now, as the problems around him have started losing their power, they have travelled inside, into the deepest corners of his mind.

All these thoughts start a tempest and it rages inside him. He does not want to look down and examine each and every part of his body, so he just looks at his own face, the part of himself that he is most comfortable with. He stands there, in front of the mirror, as if he has seen a ghost. The ghost which is standing opposite him, staring at him with a brief smile on its face, which looks more sinister than friendly. The eyes of the devil are huge and shining, and Gregor feels as if they pull him inside, into the dark world within.

Have you seen the devil?
Have you seen the devil?
The big eyes?
The small nose?
The mouth which is there,

But not there?
The long antennas
That fall down
And touch your face?
The pair of hands,
That you don't wish to see?
Have you seen the devil?
If you have, that was me
If you haven't,
I wish you would never see me.

Gregor did not see the dawn breaking, nor did he notice the first glimmer of light creeping into the room. His father, however, woke to a chilling sight—Gregor, standing motionless in front of the mirror, his face nearly pressed against the mirror. His neck was stretched unnaturally long, his bulging eyes fixed on his own reflection. He was utterly still, like a corpse held upright. For ten long seconds, Gregor's father stared in frozen disbelief, unable to comprehend what he was witnessing. The horror truly set in when he realized Gregor wasn't even breathing.

"Gregor! GREGOR!" His father's voice cracked through the silence, sharp and urgent.

Nothing. Gregor remained unmoved. For a few unbearable moments, it was as if his body were suspended in time. Then, with a slow, mechanical turn, Gregor shifted his head toward his father. His eyes, swollen and bloodshot, seemed grotesquely large, veins crawling across their surface like cracks in glass. His face was devoid of any humanity—his mouth twisted into an eerie, round 'O,' his ears pulled back and strangely enlarged, as if they no longer belonged to him.

"Gregor! What the hell is wrong with you?" his father shouted, his voice rising in panic.

Slowly, a smile spread across Gregor's face, but it was not a smile of joy. It was distorted, a triangle instead of a crescent.

Gregor's father moves forward and lands a mighty slap on his face. The slap is so powerful that Gregor falls down on the floor, passed out.

CHAPTER FOURTEEN

"I never thought I'd get to see you again."

"I think you should thank your fate," the woman in the red dress says, as she looks outside. The train has only started gaining speed. Her hair is flowing in the wind. It is a dark morning, and Gregor looks at the woman sitting opposite to him like he doesn't want to lose sight of her, ever.

"I think I should thank my father."

"Why?"

"I don't know. In some ways, I think he has helped me in arranging this meeting."

She turns to look at him.

"See," Gregor says, looking down at his own body. He lifts up his insect hand for her to see. "I'm completely an insect now. My head, hands, legs, abdomen, back, everything."

"So, now I have more reasons to love you," she says. "But..."

"But...?"

"I think we shouldn't get attached to each other. Remember the last time when you just completely disappeared from my sight?" She says.

Gregor nods. "You're right. We shouldn't get attached."

"Last time when you disappeared I just couldn't get you out of my mind."

Gregor nods. He wants to tell her, he missed her too, but he knows that that is not true.

"Let's try to hold hands?" She says, extending her insect hand towards him. He attempts to touch her, but it doesn't give any touch sensation. They hold hands although they aren't feeling anything.

She reaches her face out to kiss him, and almost touches his invisible lips as the train jolts.

"What's happening?" She takes her face back, and looks outside the window. The train is passing a bridge, and they see a river on either side.

The train jolts again, and now it is falling. Being in the river, Gregor looks at her for a final time. She seems to have no experience underwater. She is struggling to breathe, and moves her body violently. The train is now completely submerged into the water, and everything is just shades of blue and green.

CHAPTER FIFTEEN

Gregor wakes up as his father splashes water on his face. His vision is blurred, and when he looks down at his own body, he sees his body getting consumed by black currant. He feels as if he is at the waterbed with his body covered in dark green mosses. He has been in the river for so long that now he has transformed into a water plant. His father, who now seems like a big fish, with big eyes and gills, is looking down at him, and asking him something, and for Gregor, those words travel around the world, meet other words, and return back to him in unison, making it difficult for him to differentiate and comprehend each of those words, and what they mean. As words doesn't work, his father starts slapping him on his cheek, softly at first, the momentum increasing with each slap. First it is level one... level two... level three... and on the fifth level, Gregor returns back to the world. Now, Gregor's father is not a big fish with huge eyes and fins, but he is a normal human being. Gregor hits his head twice, because he is continuously feeling like he is being drawn into one dream after another. He is also having a sharp headache, because of the sleepless night. As he finally realises that he is an object of attention before his family members, he gets up from the bed, although the world is dancing around him. He is seeing dual versions of his world... His father... His mother... His sister... He feels as if the room is crowded, and he needs to wade through a group of people in order to leave the room.

He looks at his father, with his eyes oscillating from one point to other, because he isn't sure where his father actually stands, because he is now seeing so many versions of him. As he asks, "What is the time now?", he isn't actually looking at his father, but to his right.

The father hesistates, and looks at his wife and daughter before answering.

Gregor does not hear the time his father say, but he is aware that he is late for work. He wants to get up from the bed, and start preparing for work, but something in him tells that he isn't a normal human being anymore. He can't work and behave like a normal human being. But, still he has the innate need to make a performance before his family that he is alright, and nothing is going wrong with him. His father is saying something, and now it feels like someone is forcefully, with very strong and harsh hands, shutting his ears off the voices that come to him. His father shakes him by his shoulders. Gregor doesn't look up at his father and ask him what he wants, but instead, he looks down on his own body, and he sees an insect. There's no mirror in front of him, but he sees his own reflection. The face of an insect sternly looking back, with its antennas moving and touching him. He sits there, as if losing all his powers and succumbing to fate, looking at his own reflection, which does not exist, accepting defeat. He again looks at his father, like he is blind, looking to the right of his father, and asks for the time. His father tells something he can't comprehend, but according to Gregor, his father is asking him to hurry up because he is already late for work. He gets up from the bed and shoves his father away, and walks towards the bathroom. He walks using his hands as guiding sticks, and mostly using his muscle memory. His mother and sister try to get hold of him on the way, but he doesn't stop. He instead walks into the bathroom and slams the door shut.

CHAPTER SIXTEEN

"Hello, sir. Are you having a good day?"

Gregor is looking at the world that goes behind him, as the train tears through the air like a bullet. It is rather a cloudy day which makes everything dark, as if it is the day of the eclipse. Gregor, trying to suppress the million thoughts that rage inside him, can't seem to suppress the tear drops waiting for an escape. He only has a brief memory of what had happened that morning. He knows that all his family is concerned about him. They were all saying some things to him in the morning, although he couldn't understand anything, or it could be better to say that Gregor wasn't paying attention. Gregor thinks about the last time the world has revolved around him. Maybe it was a few years back. Now his world revolves around his work. Now, that is what he lives for. When he finally finds himself in a train seat, he feels strangely at peace. Now, he need not rush, the train will take him to his work, and he can stay calm. Few minutes into the train journey, Gregor falls into a meditative state, where he starts introspecting and thinking about what he had been doing, and how it had started affecting his family. All he wanted was to make his family happy, but instead he is slowly transforming into a burden for them. All these thoughts push out the emotions brimming inside him, and he tries to cover his face, and hide the tears from the other passengers. Nobody wants to see a weak man. He has forgotten to take his hat today, otherwise no one will have to see his devilish yet miserable face. He shrinks too much into himself, and tries to act as if he is sleeping, whereas his eyes are wide open to see the reality and it's brewing the fear inside him. The train is too crowded for anyone to notice Gregor, but the young man sitting opposite to Gregor's seat had his eyes on him, after asking the question. Gregor doesn't realise that the question is directed at him. He just stays in his position, trying to cover his face further.

"Sir, are you having a good day?" The man asks again, now touching Gregor on his knee. It shakes Gregor awake. He looks at the man sitting opposite him, with a clean shaven face, a pointed nose, lifeless eyes, and well combed hair. He is dressed well, as if he is also going to work. To confirm this further, he has a workers' bag hung on his shoulder. Gregor looks at him, but the man doesn't smile. He looks at Gregor as if he doesn't usually ask this question to others, which means now he is seriously concerned. He keeps looking at him with a frown, almost a stare, expecting an answer, expecting a result of his out-of-the-nature behaviour. Gregor also finds himself out of his usual character, because of this unknown person who is trying to stick his leg into his life. The face of the man sitting opposite him, was a face that demanded the truth and nothing else. Gregor is caught in a situation where he can't lie, so he doesn't speak, probably trying to act mute, so that the man would lose interest and turn away from him. Gregor also finds it difficult to break eye contact and look away. The man's face suddenly breaks into a smile, and he looks at Gregor with compassionate eyes. "I'm sorry. I didn't mean to scare you. It's ok if you don't want to talk about it."

"No. I'm just very bad at talking, and public interactions in general."

"I too am, although I am an insurance broker. I'm not myself when I work. We are neither expected to be ourselves, right?"

"And I'm working in the marketing department. Life is a real struggle these days. Life was getting better, but then..."

"Any reason for that? Did anything happen?"

Gregor looks at the man like a culprit trying to hide his crime, and shakes his head briefly.

"You can tell me. Consider me as a good friend." The man smiles softly, looks at Gregor and encourages him to speak more.

Gregor shakes his head again and shuts his mouth close as if sealing it tight. He succeeds in breaking eye contact and looks away, outside the window.

"What's stopping you? What's wrong with telling me?"

"It's just..." Gregor is out of reasons. He wonders why a stranger he just met is acting so stubbornly, and so interested in his life. What should he say? About the guy who committed suicide, right in front of him? About the fact that he thinks that he is nothing but a bug? Or should he tell about the people who bullied and traumatized him in his formative years, which includes his dear parents? Or about the work Gregor hates to do, day in and day out? Or about the pressure his family has on him to keep working and keep providing? Or about the fact that he can't be in a proper romantic relationship, and it's difficult for him to be friends with others? No, that's the silliest reason of all. Maybe he should tell him about his boss, who doesn't even give him the opportunity to breathe properly. What can be a satisfying answer, so that he will shut his mouth?

"I think it's just my work," Gregor says finally. "It's taking a toll on me." He ruffles his hair, making it look more shabby.

"Work affects each one of us," he says, leaning a bit closer towards Gregor. "I don't think that's the reason."

"Yeah. But I think that's the base of all my problems. It's simply changing the way I think about myself."

"What do you mean? What do you think about yourself now?"

"I worked so hard, with all dedication, tried to be better than everyone else, tried to be in the market; I tried so hard to impress my boss; I think I worked so hard, that finally I've become like an insect; An insect that no one likes, an insect that no one wants; an insect that has lost its way from other insects, and had to live with humans; an insect that is not useful to anyone anymore; a fragile insect living and simply waiting for its blissful natural death, or a painful death due to the wounds on its body that never heal. Believe me. This is all that's going on. I've said the truth. Please don't ask me anything else."

The man sitting opposite to him suddenly feels so heavy, seeing the emotional outburst, and has no words to say. He leans back and looks outside the window. One watching him will even doubt whether he is breathing. But Gregor is still looking at him with eyes that are ready to tear through the man's heart. Gregor feels like he has transferred his sorrow to this young man, or maybe the word shared would be a better usage, because Gregor still feels the weight of it. Two men are sitting on opposite sides, inside a crowded train, thinking that it's awkward to get close, hug each other and cry their hearts out. Gregor only wants the train to stop, so that he can get out and continue to live the lie that he has been living, a life away from truth and people who demand it. Truth is bitter. Truth is weird.

"I am sorry," Gregor says and touches the knee of the man.

The man looks at Gregor and smiles. "No it's ok. I didn't expect this. When I demanded the truth, you just killed me with words."

Gregor laughs for the first time in many days. "You speak like a writer."

"I am one. Besides being an insurance broker."

"Really? What do you write? Poems? Stories?"

"Some insignificant novels and short stories, mostly," he says, smiling. "I write for myself, to give an outlet to the weirdness in me. Sometimes, I feel like burning them all... all these bizarre, weird stories... I don't think anyone will want to read these. There are better novels out there people would like to spend their time on."

"Bizarre and weird... Life is bizarre and weird."

"But, that's not what most people expect to read in novels, you know? They don't want a writer to put an axe on their frozen minds, although that's what novels should be capable of. If we are reading only to make our lives better, then why choose books? There are thousands of other ways to be happy. Why books, even?"

"Nonsense," Gregor says.

"If you write a novel that pleases everyone, then you sure are not writing anything significant. Such novels bring you money, but nothing more comes out of it. A good novel should do nothing but wake you up with a mighty blow on your head, so that we start thinking differently. When I see people attacking writers because a certain group of people are offended, I feel like those writers are on the right path."

"People who like these romances and fantasies might have a different story to tell," Gregor says.

"They sure do. But, I think people don't want writers like me. They want to hear lies that make them happy."

"Since there is a writer to write all these, there should definitely be a bunch of people who want to read such books."

"But, I have never written anything, just to impress someone or cater to the needs of some group of people. A good writer should write for themselves, and for the betterment of the world. Some idiots would think that we make the world a better place by shutting off the negativity around us. It is like meditating in peace, or based on history, playing the fiddle, while the whole world around you is burning. We should rather put ourselves into that fire and save people trapped within those flames, or even take some efforts to put that fire out. Playing the fiddle is comfortable, latter is not. No wonder people choose that path."

"But, all these efforts of writers will go into waste if nobody reads them."

"People will recognise me some day," he says. "I just write because I can't stop myself from writing. Otherwise I would've stopped. I would've stopped everything. There is still something inside me that asks me to keep living."

"You should write," Gregor says. "You should live."

"I say all these sad things to go back home, and start writing another weird novel. Maybe, I am going to imagine you as an insect. You know, from what you just shared with me."

"Don't do that," Gregor says. He leans forward from his resting position and looks at the man with concern. The man looks at Gregor for a second and turns his face towards the window.

"Don't worry, no one's going to read it anyways." He laughs.

Gregor falls back on his seat. "It's just a weird concept. Don't even attempt writing it. No one will ever read it."

"But tell me," the man says, turning his gaze at Gregor. "Is that not the truth?"

Gregor frowns. "I just used that word insect figuratively, man. Not literally. If you write something like that, that sure is going to be really weird, and nobody will even care to buy that book in the first place."

"You just told me that there might still be some people who will read my works. My novels are weird, very absurd like the theme I just shared with you. Also my novels are so absurd that nobody is gonna think that it is based on a true story," the man laughs again, briefly.

"It is not a true story. You are just trying to write a novel based on a metaphor." Gregor goes silent then, because in his mind he is aware that it is not simply a theme for a story, but his life. But, he doesn't want to talk more about his life with this man. He is unsure what more resources he will collect from their conversation, that would point towards himself.

"What's your name?" Gregor asks.

"You can call me Frank," he says. "What's yours?"

"You can call me Gregor."

"Is that your real name?" The man says with his usual laughter.

"Don't worry about that."

The train slowly comes to a halt, and the man gets up, adjusting his bag and overcoat.

"We'll meet some other time," he says.

Gregor waves at him, and the man disappears from sight.

CHAPTER SEVENTEEN

During his time in the office, Gregor has never once felt like he was being part of something bigger than himself. He goes to work, finishes all the tasks given to him with utmost dedication, counts days, and receives a decent amount of salary on the same date, at the beginning of every month. Besides that, he doesn't know where his works go; what his boss receives from it; or what the true aim of the company is. People, even his boss, advise him not to work for money. "If money is your only concern, you can quit your job today. If what you want is self-improvement, then you can remain here," his boss had said in the first few days. The boss had asked Gregor if he was working for money and Gregor had shook his head and said no. But money is the only reason why he was here and that's the only reason why he would keep working, without even knowing who, or what he is working for.

Today, just as Gregor is about to start the day, his marketing team gets called into the boss's cabin for another meeting. Gregor braces himself, and this time he doesn't forget to take his water bottle, so that he will not go dehydrated; he doesn't want another day of headache; another day of mania.

Gregor sits on the chair like an obedient child, keeping his water bottle to himself, wondering whether or not he can keep the bottle on the boss's table. But he just looks at his boss, waiting for him to open his mouth.

The boss has a slow way of starting a meeting. He takes all the time in the world, and lags the whole situation like a sleepy movie. He takes a few sips of his green tea, relaxes himself on his chair, with the top of his abdomen going above his head. He smiles at all of them present; a smile so pleasant that it can easily be misunderstood. He smiles specifically at Gregor and asks him how he is. Gregor says that he is fine, returning the smile. Gregor's smile is so feeble and non-existent that if the boss had asked the question again, then he would have cried. But when Gregor says "I'm fine," the boss turns his gaze towards the other members present. He has a smile on his face as if he is a spiritual Guru who has just come out of a week-long meditation.

"Alright" the boss says and the meeting starts. Gregor finds it difficult to be attentive and concentrate on what the boss was saying. He feels like the words are getting jumbled; the words and the sentences lack meaning. But he looks at the boss and nods his head as if he understands what the boss is trying to say. Gregor catches certain phrases from the boss like "promotional event", "day after tomorrow", "need to talk to people", "posters and banners", and finally the boss changes his tone into that of urgency (which prompts Gregor to be more awake and it kind of wakes up Gregor from a dream he was in) and tells them, "All of these works need to be done very fast. The event is the day after tomorrow. Prepare all the posters, banners and forms, and make plans to make this program a success. It depends on all of us, and how much effort we put in. There's no time to waste."

Today, there is no meaningless talks about totally unrelated things, so the meeting ends rather fastly. Although Gregor was exploring the wonderland along with Alice, in the end he was able to understand what the boss was trying to say, and the pace at which he should be working. Gregor walks out of the boss's cabin and returns to his cabin, resolved to start working. Gregor has only rested his body on the chair, when he gets called back to the boss's cabin. He walks into the room, and realises that the facial expression of the boss has changed.

"Gregor, what the fuck are you trying to do?" The boss asks and Gregor looks at him with a confused face. "You look like a drug addict. It's as if you just returned from jail, after getting arrested for drug peddling. Atleast get your beard shaved for fuck's sake, and get your hair cut. Day after tomorrow is an important event and you should look presentable and talk to those people very well. Don't you need this job? If you don't want to work then you can leave today. Don't test my patience ever again. Tomorrow when you come to the office, you need to look presentable, you get me? And why the hell are your eyes getting welled up like a child? If you can't control your emotions, then find some other job, work under someone else, not under me. I am like this."

"I'm sorry sir," Gregor says.

"Go."

Gregor walks back to his seat and wipes off the tears that had almost came out of his eyes. He covers his face, and tries to make it look composed, and starts with his work.

CHAPTER EIGHTEEN

Gregor stands outside the hair salon, watching the closed shop where he had seen the teenagers, last month. The hair salon is crowded in the evening, and when Gregor checked his phone to watch reels, he found that he was running out of battery, so he decided to stand there and look at the closed shop to see any movements. The night is calmer than ever, and a cold wind edges past him, as if trying to knock him down, rustling his hair, and his shirt which is tucked out from the pants. He has his overcoat on his shoulders, and his hat on the other. There is a guy standing next to him in the village attire, blowing a cigarette. Gregor hated people who blew out cigarette smoke like the whole world belonged to them. He used to move away from them and stare at them from a distance, as if they were doing a huge sin. But now, Gregor just stands there, unmoved breathing in the smoke and polluting his lungs. He doesn't know if passive smoking is as effective as real smoking, but he knows that the former does more harm than the latter. Gregor looks at the man standing next to him and smirks. The man smiles back. Gregor turns his gaze away from him and looks at the closed shop. He checks the watch, and finds that it is not time yet. Gregor stands there covered in smoke, patient yet impatient. He looks through the glass doors of the hair salon. There are two chairs and both of them are occupied, and two crimpers are working on each one of them. They take an unusually long time to get their hair and beard trimmed, before they wait for a face massage. Gregor looks at the crimper who usually worked on his hair. He is a gentle and understanding man, who has the unusual skill to perfectly decode what Gregor wants. Gregor only needs to give him a few prompts and he will cut the hair exactly as he wanted it. That is the reason why Gregor frequents this shop, and does not go anywhere else.

"Gregor, you are late this time," the crimper says as he helps Gregor settle on the barber chair. "Look at how your hair has grown. You have started growing a beard too. It's unusual."

Gregor is confused as to what he must say. It has been five days since Gregor has actually seen his face. When he looks into the mirror, all he sees is an insect head staring back at him. How is he supposed to see that his hair has out grown him, or that he has started growing a beard?

Gregor just smiled the remark off. "Don't keep the beard, shave it off, and trim the sides off my head, but don't go too much on the middle part."

"Like usual?"

"Like usual."

Gregor wants to tell the crimper about the promotional event that is going to take place on the day after tomorrow and that he has to look presentable, but, the social battery of Gregor has already ran out, and the crimper has already started with his work, and Gregor does not want to disturb him. The crimper takes the electric trimmer, and starts working on Gregor's hair. Gregor has one accidental look at the mirror, and he sees the huge insect head. He immediately takes his glance from the mirror, and tries to distract himself by looking sideways, and then, when he realises that he is still able to see his face from the hindsight, he closes his eyes. The music comes out through the huge speakers that are kept on the side. Gregor wonders why people like sad romantic songs. Gregor always avoided them; he hurriedly skips one, when it arrives during shuffled music plays. But tonight, he realises that he has no choice but to put through this torture, since he had to get the haircut done, by whatever means. Gregor tries to concentrate his ears to the minute sound of the scissors clipping the hair, and keep the song to the backdrop as much as possible. That's when he hears a huge crashing sound on the road. The scissors stop cutting, and the crimper rushes to the door, and opens it to see what is going on. Gregor opens his eyes and looks in that direction.

"It is those reckless teenagers again," he says, as he shuts the door, and comes back to Gregor. "None of them are in their senses. Drugs... Alcohol... What not? They are doing bike stunts on the road, as if this is a circus. Let them die with their own hands; we don't care anymore."

Gregor is silent. His eyes are everywhere except the mirror, and in one oblivious moment, he looks at it; at his own face. He remembers that night when he encountered those teenagers. The arguments... The fight... The girl who had asked the guys to be easy on him... The fall... The pain... As he realises that his mind is in a different place, he returns back to reality, and his insect head comes into his focus. He does not shut his eyes and he rather looks at his face, and feels like he is being hypnotized. Even when the crimper moves his head, to the left and right, top and bottom for cutting the hair, and shaving his beard, he does not wake up from the dream he is having with his eyes open. He finds himself caught in a spiral, that was turning slowly, and he is being pulled into it.

"Gregor!" The crimper shakes him, and that is when he wakes up, as if from an afternoon nap. "Seems you were lost in thought." He laughs.

"Yeah. Sorry about that."

"Is it ok?"

Gregor looks at the crimper doubtfully. "Is what ok?"

"Your face Gregor. Do you want me to make any changes, or is this fine with you?"

"Oh you are asking about my hair cut?"

"Yeah. What else?"

Gregor examines his face in the mirror, and all he sees is the insect head. He is not even sure whether his hair is actually trimmed. He looks at his face for a few seconds in worry, and then turns towards the crimper. "Yeah, the haircut is perfect, as always. Did you shave my beard?"

"Gregor, can't you see it in the mirror?"

"Just answer my question, godammit."

The crimper glares at him for a brief moment. "Why are you getting so worked up, huh?"

"Just... I am asking you a simple question... Just give me an answer for that. I don't want to have an argument with you."

The crimper is silent, his ego not letting him speak.

Gregor brings his hands to his face, and runs it through his chin, and beneath his nose, to find that there is no single hair on it. But, on the mirror, Gregor finds himself touching on his insect head, and that sends shockwaves through his chest.

"I am sorry," Gregor says.

Gregor gets up from the chair, pays the crimper and walks out of the salon. As Gregor is on the way back to his home, he feels as if he is still moving through a spiral. He barely sees the teenagers who are revving up their bikes. They do not disturb him as he passes them with unsteady steps, like an inebriated man. Gregor forgets where he is going, although finally he reaches his home. He mechanically gets freshened up. He barely hears whatever his parents and sister say, so he does not give them any answer. He comes to his bedroom and falls on his bed, as he got pulled into it. He is still trapped in that spiral, and in the dream, he was falling more and more into it. It is as if he is falling into a pit that has no end.

That night Gregor sees weird and horrific dreams. He sees those dreams with open eyes. Through the dim light that seeps into the room, Gregor sees the ceiling fan which is spiralling at full speed above him. For a second with sudden shock, he sees the body of a huge insect hanging on it, dead. He imagines the scenes that will possibly happen tomorrow if such a thing were real. When his parents and his sisters open the door to his room, they will not see Gregor on the bed, but a huge insect which has succumbed to the tortures of its mind. Tonight, something tells inside him that it is the end; tonight is the day his world and all its tortures will finally come to an end. But something does not let him get up from the bed and make that fatal decision. It is not a force which is kind and unknown. But it is repressive and nails him to the bed with harsh boots at the ends of his limbs, and his forehead. Suddenly darkness binds him, and he feels a weight on his chest, as if someone is sitting on top of him. The hands are suffocating him and covering his mouth, which does not allow him to scream for help. Although his nostrils are covered, he is able to smell green apples around him. The odour intensifies, and it travels into him, coursing through all of his neural pathways.

And five minutes before he wakes up, he sleeps.

Santa Claus

CHAPTER NINETEEN

Today is a beautiful day!

Gregor is never afraid of nightmares, at least he never was. Sometimes, when he didn't see a nightmare, he used to get disappointed and pray to God to give him a nightmare that night. He loved that feeling when he went through a nightmare and woke up terrified but with a sense of relaxation that it was all a dream. There was nothing in the world that made him happy like a nightmare. He dodged all problems that came his way in real life, but he loved having problematic dreams. Nightmares are like a friend who plays extreme pranks, only to reveal it in the end, as if it was the biggest joke. Sometimes, he hopes that his life itself would be concluded as an elaborate prank and someone would come to reveal that he actually lived a happy life somewhere else. He loved nightmares. Maybe that's the reason why nightmares became a part of his life even during the day-time when he was wide awake.

Gregor gets out of his bed and walks out of the room, to the hall. He has a brief glance at his father who was on the sofa, scrolling through his phone for the daily news. Father looks up at him. His face changes expression and a frown is slowly carved on it. "What happened to your face?" He asks.

"What?" Gregor runs his fingers through the face. His fingers tell him that there are scars on his face in different places; on his cheeks, chin and forehead. He runs his fingers down to his neck and finds that there are scratches on the neck too. Gregor feels his nails with his other fingers. It is grown, and he finds dirt under them. He wonders if it was only his own skin tissue.

"I think this happened while I was sleeping," Gregor says.

"This is not normal." His father's eyes narrow.

"No. It is usual. Nothing to worry about," Gregor says as he walks to the bathroom, not giving his father a chance to interrogate him further.

He shuts the world off and stands in front of the mirror, avoiding his own reflection. He pulls his shirt off, and looks down at his body. What he sees is not skin and flesh, but the body of an insect that clings onto him, refusing to let him find peace.

Every inch of his body radiates a dull ache, punctuated by sharp stings. His fingers roam over his chest, abdomen and back. Each touch sends a jolt of pain to his brain, making him realise he is tracing over scratches etched into his skin, raw and tender.

He unhooks his pants and lets them fall to the floor, and he's but a miserable human being forced to walk in the most grotesque fancy dress that nobody wants themselves in.

Gregor bends down and surfs his fingers through his legs, thighs, and feet, and he rarely finds any inch without wounds. "Fuck!" He mutters as he faces the bathroom wall. He rises and turns the shower on, water cascading down with a relentless force. He plants his hands on the walls and weeps silently. Just a random bug on the bathroom wall, crying its heart out.

The shower washes down his tears and strangely he feels fresh. He turns off the shower and grabs the nail cutter and starts cutting his nails. He feels the sharp pain as he cuts through his flesh, since he can't see what he is doing. Invisible insects are still surrounding his ears, making him lose focus.

Gregor washes his fingers, and touches through them realising that he has injured himself. His body is now in a confused state, unsure of where the pain is coming from.

He washes off the invisible blood, dresses himself, hiding the wounds all over his body and gets out of the bathroom, as he is well aware that he is getting late.

Gregor combs his hair without looking at the mirror, tucks in his shirt, wears the watch, gathers his earphone and mobile from his table, and walks towards the kitchen, where his mother is working.

"Mother," Gregor says, as she turns back.

She smiles at Gregor, which is her own way of wishing him goodmorning. But her smile does not last longer, as she sees the scars on his face.

"What ha-" she starts.

"It's from the sleep," he says and immediately jumps to the topic. "Look at my finger. Does it look bad?" Gregor extends his left hand and she gets hold of it. She finds that the tips of two of his fingers were injured, and she starts again, raising her voice a bit now.

"It is still bleeding! Why are you so careless?"

"I was just cutting my nails and this happened."

"Don't you even know how to cut your nails? Are you still a small child?"

"It was just an accident," he snaps. "Don't blame me for that."

"Go sit on that chair," she says, pointing at the only chair in the kitchen. Gregor walks to the chair, taking all the time in the world, while his mother rushes to the cupboard to get the first aid kit. She returns with the first aid kit and a beaker filled with cold water. She takes his hand and dips the fingers in the water.

"What's going on with you?" She asks as she wipes the water off his fingers with a cloth. "You don't seem good at all."

Gregor is silent. He hates lying to his mother, so whenever he is in a position where the truth is undesirable, he just stays silent.

"Gregor, you are more aware of it than me, right? What's wrong? Tell me. I promise you that no one else will know about it."

"I cannot make you understand," Gregor says with a sharp look, his expressions changing with every word he utters. "I cannot make anyone understand what is happening inside me. I cannot even explain it to myself."

His mother stops working on his wounds and looks up at him for a while. She finds that the calm features of his face have suddenly metamorphosed into that of agony, with the folds on his forehead huge and embossed. Two seconds later his face slowly fades into the calm features and a smile gets painted on his face.

She notices this change but gets back to the wound, as if she wasn't paying attention. "The other day, your father was talking about meeting some psychologists or shrinks. But trust me Gregor, nobody will understand you better than your mother," she says in a relaxed tone, not looking up.

"It's way beyond your comprehension."

"So, you think you know what's the limit of my comprehension?" She says, as she ties up the bandage. "Just tell me. I'm sure that's what you want at this moment."

Gregor throws one last glance at his mother and gets up from the chair. He gets the plate, collects his breakfast and walks to the dining table.

CHAPTER TWENTY

Christmas is barely a week away. The railway station is decorated in red, white and green. It is rather crowded, and people are talking and laughing as if the Christmas spirits have already gotten into them. To his right, he sees Santa Clauses standing as a group, and discussing something, and they wave at him as he passes them. Gregor acknowledges them with a brief smile. As he passes them, he turns back to look at them, with a childish curiosity, to know whether they are real Santa Clauses. But he finds no reason to think that they are not. To his left he sees the reindeers and sleighs being parked. The reindeers are probably taking rest, getting themselves ready to accept the busy life that arrives with Christmas. Gregor notices the train which is parked in the station, which is not his train, and he finds with surprise that the colours of the train have changed from blue and orange to gold and brown. The train is also decorated with carvings and sculptures of animal heads, including sheep and donkeys. A kind of thick smoke is coming from underneath the train, making it look like the vehicle is standing on top of a cloud. Gregor watches all of this with his mouth agape. But he also notices with curiosity that no one in the railway station seems surprised like him. He looks at the people as if he is asking them to leave everything behind and look at this marvel, but it seems Gregor is the only one who is intrigued by it. Passengers are going in and out of the train, and they show no surprise either. He stands there wondering how people these days have become unromantic and indifferent. But, he knows that something is off. This is not how a group of people would behave when something out of the ordinary happens. It's time the group of people should be mobbing around the Santa Clauses, clicking photographs, videos and taking selfies without respecting their personal space. Instead these people behave as if this is a normal happening. Even the kids present are not curious about the Santa Clauses and reindeers, or the fancy looking train that seems to move through clouds. Gregor feels too tired anyway. Every inch of his body is in pain, and last night he barely slept for five minutes. He knows instead of thinking about the things that happen around him, he should be thinking about himself; his body, his mental health. These days he has even started forgetting that he has a body and mind. Instead of thinking why the mind of other people works the way it does, he should start thinking about his own mind, and why it is becoming so weird these days. Gregor makes that decision, and he starts watching the world with a sense of indifference and contempt; when everything is going wrong with oneself, who cares about Santa Clauses, reindeers and fancy trains? But Gregor cares, although he does not. Gregor forcefully keeps those fancy things out of his mind and decides to wait for his train, so that he can finally find some rest in the train.

Gregor finds that he is earlier than usual. He feels so sleepy that it seems to him that he might fall down. He inches towards a waiting bench and finds a spot in the corner. He plugs in his earphones and takes out his mobile phone to pass the time. When he looks up from his mobile screen for a second, he finds the world before him in a blur. The colours, the reds, the yellows, the blues, the whites and the blacks, all combining into one frame, creating images which have no meaning. For a moment, he feels like he should take some minutes of rest on the railway track, and watch the train go over him; through him. He tries to push those thoughts away and let himself be distracted by pixels and bites. It helps to an extent in calming his nerves and those voices in his head, asking him of different things at once; that he is already getting late for work; and that he should kill himself. Two girls are standing to his right now, and they are talking about someone named Ann Rudy. "Ann Rudy... Ann Rudy... Ann Rudy... Ann Rudy... Ann Rudy..." That is the only thing he hears in the conversation. He wants to listen to it; Who is Ann Rudy and why are they talking about her? But his mind is on everything and it is everywhere all at once. He is no more sure whether the girls are talking about an Ann Rudy. Maybe he is mishearing things. Maybe even those girls do not know who Ann Rudy is. "Ann Rudy... Yeah, nobody liked what she did... It was terrible, right?" No matter how high Gregor keeps the volume in his earphones, he is still hearing those pair of nouns. Ann Rudy. Who is Ann Rudy? What in the world did she do? Gregor now has a feeling like he has heard this name somewhere before. Maybe it is that woman in the red dress, that Gregor saw few days ago. Ann Rudy. She did look like an Ann Rudy. But didn't she die? It was a train crash. Or did she survive that tragedy? Maybe these girls are talking about her death, and her misfortune. Who knows; and who cares? But Gregor still remembers her final words. She spoke as if she was speaking from afar; as if in a phone call. He still remembers seeing her drowning; seeing her bright face, now covered in a hue of greenish blue. Her feeble and trembling voice said thus: *Don't forget me... I... I love you.... Can you hear me?* In the background Gregor heard the sirens of ambulances and fire engines. *I'm sorry. Goodbye.* Those words fade into eternity like a breath in the underwater.

He wants to ask the girls to stop talking about Ann Rudy, or stop talking at all, because no matter what they are saying, it somehow reaches his ears as some gossip on Ann Rudy. Gregor is not someone you see who stands up to people and asks them to stop talking, instead he is someone you will never see even if he stands right in front of your eyes. He gets up from the waiting bench, although he is feeling dizzy, and he walks to the edge of the platform with uneven steps. The train which was parked there before is gone now, and when he looks at the railway track, he sees the decorations of a Christmas tree which unusually smells bad. The focus of his eyes goes on and off, as if the unsteady lens of a camera. No matter what happens in your life; no matter what trajectory it takes; no matter how bad the mind games are; there are some people who wants nothing less than the best from you, and you need to cater to their needs no matter what. Although these people themselves can't always be perfect; although they are very well aware that one can't always be at their best, they still expect it from you. When Gregor does not feel perfect, he acts perfect. He stands tall, tightening his tie, looking at the eyes, with a confident smile playing on his lips, although he is nothing but hollow inside; the smile is nothing but a red decoration ball on a Christmas tree, without a leaf or an interior, that can break into two even in a small breeze. The brief smile broadens on his face when he hears the siren of the train from afar. It is on time today. He looks at his watch and at the direction in which his train will come. People start collecting their luggage and walk towards the platform. They rush around him, pushing him, trying to be the first person to get into the train. Gregor usually stand idly letting others push him as if he was trapped amidst huge waves, and wait for his chance to get into the train. But that day, he pushes those people back, and is the first person to enter the train. He really wants a seat today, otherwise he will collapse.

CHAPTER TWENTY-ONE

Gregor finds it with horror that no matter how tired or sleepy he is, he can't close his eyes.

It was three in the morning.

A poem he wrote probably five or six years back starts playing in his mind.

And demons came to devour my sleep.

It is a memory that he had tried his best to forget; is still trying to forget but still it returns to him at unexpected points in life. He sits by the train window, watching the world go back, and he feels as if he himself is going back in time.

His sharp fingers kept my eyelids from kissing each other.

He remembers being in a library, sitting next to a girl, looking at a piece of paper she gave him. It was a drawing. Gregor was confused. So many thoughts came to him. The painting was nothing less than horrific.

He showed me horrors of my past.

He knew that she wasn't doing well, mentally. They have had talks about it in the past. There were nights Gregor had given up his sleep for her, listening to her talk, mainly about her aspirations and hopes.

And uncertainties of my future.

She was that charming, hardworking girl that everyone loved, but there was someone she loved more than that, and that was Gregor. She had shared things with him that she has never told anyone. In her final days, what affected her more than the fact that she was dying, was the fear that she would have to leave him forever.

And kept me awake.

That day, almost five months before she died, they were in the library. She had her usual smile, when she gave him this piece of drawing. *It looks weird right?* She said laughing. *I know.* Gregor was trying to read her through what she had drawn. *Give me your book,* Gregor said. *A poem comes to my mind.*

When I turned to look at him,

Gregor wrote the poem and gave it to her. She had clapped her hands. I didn't know you could write such a beautiful poem spontaneously. Her face was so bright and red. Gregor knew that she wasn't happy, or maybe she was; it was more difficult than anything to read her face. She has even told him personally that, when she smiles, it was nothing but a pretence to fool others into thinking that she is okay.

His eyes looked so cruel yet happy.

Now that demon has come to him, to devour his sleep and mind. But, it doesn't have that devilish shape and smile as drawn by her, in her multiple drawings. Instead, it is the insect head that forms gradually before his eyes, when he stares sharply into eternity.

His vision is slightly blurred, and he starts to wonder if he is slowly losing his eyesight. He only sees the greens, blues and reds from the outside. Something prompts him to look away from the window, and divert it to the other side, to the side of the passengers. He clears his eyes and the world around him gets clearer. When he looks in front of him, he sees the woman in the red dress, sitting opposite. She was smiling at him, as if she had been smiling at him for a long time. Gregor smiles at her back. When he looks at the person sitting next to her, he finds that he is someone dressed in black attires, reading a newspaper wearing small glasses. When he observes more, he sees that it is not a human, but a bear. Gregor smiles in fascination and is not afraid of how cruel a bear can be. When he looks back at the woman in red dress, he finds her breaking into a mirth, probably upon seeing the happiness on his face. A slow and calm song is flowing through his earphones. He turns towards the window and closes his eyes. A day can seem boring and monotonous due to our dull mind, and the unhappy thoughts and memories that interject between us and the beauty of the world. But in retrspection, we see the world as it is, and how splendid it actually is. Although it is a day that is disturbed by random thoughts and memories, it is also a day he saw the railway station in a new attire. He saw the Santa Clauses and the reindeers and sleighs, although the kids were not happy about it. He saw Ann Rudy, the woman in the red dress, and finally came to know that she isn't dead, and she hasn't yet lost that sunrise smile she always carried. He saw a big bear sitting calmly in a train, reading newspaper through its tiny glasses. What more can he ask of a day. He has seen many beautiful things; although they only exist in his imagination; although two other passengers, and a few people and dogs in the railway station felt their privacy being intruded by his observatory glances. Maybe it is the bear, or it is the woman, or it is everything altogether, including the fact that he is tired, he feels sleepy, and just ten minutes into the journey, Gregor sleeps.

Regardless of anything, today is actually a beautiful day.

CHAPTER TWENTY-TWO

Gregor continues to see those characters throughout the day, at different places in the office. When he walked into the cafeteria, he saw the bear sitting at one of the tables with earphones plugged in, and laughing so hard at his mobile phone. He was probably watching some "bear fails", Gregor imagined. When he opened the fridge, to get some chilled mineral water, and closed it, the woman in the red dress was standing by the door, with her right hand on her hip and left hand extending a soft drink can. Gregor was spooked.

"Coca cola?" She asked.

"I don't drink that," Gregor said.

"You must be a Ronaldo fan."

"What?"

"I don't want to explain it to you," she said.

"I don't watch football these days."

"Cricket?"

"No."

"Basketball?"

"No."

"Olympics?"

"No."

"Chess?"

"No."

"Porn?"

Gregor started to say "no" with the flow of it, but then he stopped and glared at her, as if she had asked a condemnable question that needed no answer.

"Why are you here? You're only supposed to be in my dream." He said, looking at her insect hand. "In the morning, you were on the train. Now you're in the office. I'm starting to suspect that you're stalking me."

"Wait, are you trying to flirt with me, now? Really? In your dreams? And what's this nonsense of stalking you on a fucking train? I haven't even travelled on a train since I was like eight years old. Also, I have worked in this office for the last three years. Can't I be expected to be found here?" She said, her voice raising a bit.

"Past three years? No way. Cus I've never seen you around."

"You're a crazy workaholic bitch. How will you ever see me?" She said looking at him, and then he realised that he had upsetted her. So he remained quiet, as if his lips were sealed. "I was literally having a good day. I only offered you a cola and you just ruined my day from every corner possible. You know what-" Her voice faded off. She was looking at the glass window that separated the office space from the cafeteria. He found her frozen for a moment. Her eyes were widened, as if she was looking at a monster.

"What happened?" Gregor said, as he turned back to the glass window.

His boss was looking back at him, as if he was ready to eat him up. Gregor frowned at his boss and turned back to the woman in the red dress, without any change in expression. "Why is Santa Claus here? Is there a celebration today?"

The woman in the red dress stared at him for a brief moment, and got out of the cafeteria. Gregor watched her go, and his gaze again fell on the Santa Clause, who was still staring at him with sharp eyes. Gregor then saw his own reflection at the glass window, and it hurt him a bit.

"Gregor, come to my office now!" The Santa Clause roared.

The familiar terrifying voice hit him forcefully on his face. The Santa Clause image fell off and he had a sudden realisation of who it was.

Saying that, his boss walked towards his office.

Gregor slapped his head in despair, got out of the cafeteria, and followed his boss to the office, with fear enveloping him like a chilling breeze.

CHAPTER TWENTY-THREE

That's where the hallucinations seemed to end. It is like someone has pulled him back to the real world by his collar.

As he walks to the boss's office, he sees a woman from the workspace, staring at him, less with anger and more with sympathy. He assumes that she was the girl he had talked to in the cafeteria; the girl he had assumed to be the woman in the red dress, who only visited him in his dreams. These are the moments of realization, and he knows that his job is at stake for some reason, although he has not done anything wrong.

When he enters his boss's office, he finds the huge man on his executive chair trying to relax himself. He asks Gregor to take the seat in front of him. Gregor obeys.

"Gregor, I don't want to be angry at you. I'm trying not to be," he says, with a smile on his lips. "I also don't want to ask you to go back to your normal introverted state and focus only on your work. Because I know that you need some relaxation too. We can't always work, right? But, today is not the right day for that. As you know, tomorrow is an important day. A major event is coming up, and I want your concentration to remain only on that. Also, if you get some spare time, prepare what you should tell the new potential customers. Don't shift your focus towards unimportant things. So far you are doing it well, and today, we might have to work overtime. So, just keep that in mind, and be careful not to waste company time. Okay?"

Gregor nods. "Ok, sir. Got it."

"But, why didn't you take my call? That's what angered me. That's why I shouted at you by the cafeteria. When I checked the

CCTV, I saw you wasting company time. That's the reason why I ringed you. But you ignored the calls."

Gregor takes his phone out of his pocket, and finds that there are two missed calls from him. "I am sorry, sir. I didn't see the calls."

"Okay. Now get back to your work. Don't upset me again. Ever. Okay?"

Gregor nods and walks out of the cabin.

CHAPTER TWENTY-FOUR

Gregor dies everyday. He is like a caterpillar working day in and out, feeding on leaves, hanging upside down, all to build a cocoon. But instead of metamorphosing into a butterfly, he falls dead to the soil, only to be reborn as a cicada. This is his life-cycle.

He finds himself curled up into a corner, with his hands on his legs, taking up as little space as possible, looking outside the train window, looking at darkness; at nothing. He wears the hats, and tries not to look at anyone around him; or not to invite suspicious glances towards him, although he inadvertently is doing the exact same thing.

Some time into the train journey, only to distract himself from his own thoughts, he takes out his phone, and starts scrolling reels. He finds that bugs have even taken over his Instagram feeds. It is as if the world is conspiring itself to put him into this situation. Nevertheless, he scrolls away such reels, and only watch what interests him.

That is when he receives a WhatsApp notification from his sister. He immediately opens it. It was a video, he takes time to download it, and waits for it patiently. He plays the video and increases the volume. It is a music video, where his sister is playing the violin, along with people playing other instruments inside a room. Gregor never used to take it seriously when he sees her sister goes out every weekend to learn violin. But nevertheless, he supported it. He bought her the violin first year into his job, and he still continues to pay for her violin classes. He never thought that she was actually benefiting from those classes, and she was possible to create something as beautiful as what he listens to now. A smile forms on his lips, accidentally. He doesn't know how many times he has replayed it, but he also finds with surprise that he is unable to stop smiling. But he does not give a reply to it, he does not even react with a love emoji to that video. Probably he will say something when he sees her in person, but usually he never appreciated her for anything; like the primary instinct of most brothers, he only teased her, although he secretly roots for her. But, nevertheless, even after the number of times he had watched that video has reached its saturation point, he still continues to watch and it nurtured the smile on his lips. That is when a call notification popped up. It is from an unknown number. Although Gregor never likes to attend phone calls, he takes every single call that arrives on his phone for the last three years, afraid that it may be somehow related to his work.

Gregor takes the phone call. A female voice comes from the other end. "Hello? Gregor?"

"Yes. Who is it?"

"I'm Meera, from work. Today, we were talking about Coca Cola and created a controversy."

"Let's not put the blame on Coca Cola. And yes. I am really sorry for what happened."

Meera laughs briefly. "Actually no, I must say sorry to you. You got called into the cabin, because of me."

"No need, because I am the one who is to take blame for that."

"Why can't you just take an apology, you dumbass?" Her voice raises.

Gregor is silent, unsure of what to say or how to react.

"I am sorry again. Just take my apology, and let's not talk about it again."

"Yes sure."

"Say you accepted my apology."

Gregor is silent for a second, and then he thinks that she will cut the call if he says those words. "Yes. I have accepted your apology."

"Thanks."

Gregor is silent again.

"Are you always like this?" She asks.

"Like what?"

"Never mind," she says and hangs up the call, the beep sound piercing through his ears, which continues to stay, even after a few seconds. Gregor was not feeling lonely before, but after Meera has cut the call, he feels as if loneliness has started eating him, from his toes. That is when his phone vibrates again. It was a call from the same number as before.

"Hello," Gregor says.

"Yeah, hello. Sorry for hanging up on you. My anger issues are bad these days. Excuse me for that."

"It's ok."

"No, it's not. All these unexpressed anger at work and home, maybe. Today morning, I literally felt like killing you. I would have, if it wasn't for the boss."

Gregor is silent again. He wants to know more about that. But he doesn't ask, because he knows that he hasn't reached that level of intimacy.

"I have a sad life when you start thinking about it," she laughs. "No, I actually called you to apologize, and to ask you what happened inside the cabin. That's why I called again. What did sir say? Did he tell you anything about me?"

"No, he didn't. He actually talked softly, and asked me to just focus on my work, atleast for today. You know, tomorrow's program?"

"Yeah. I know about it. But, I don't think that is the reason why he called you."

"Then?"

"He is an insecure ass and a fucking pervert. He just didn't like it when he saw you talking to me, through his stupid CCTV. And he wanted to show his power, right in front of me, by shouting at you. You won't understand it, but I understood it clearly well. I saw all of that in that single look he gave me. And, as we argued just now, it is not my fault or yours. It is his fault. You know, he is the biggest pervert I have ever worked with."

Gregor is at a lack of words. He is too stunned to speak.

"And you say, he talked softly? All those things are just a facade. He wears the most expensive mask in the office, dude."

"All these seem new to me."

"It's not smooth for anyone, dude," she says. "Do you remember his G-Mail ID?" Her words gain speed, almost turning into a funny tone.

"manucrown@gmail.com?"

"Yeah," she laughs. "I was thinking the other day that his name should be Manu Clown. Because, that is all he is. A fucking clown."

A sudden burst of laughter comes out of him, but he immediately stops it and maintains a straight face, because the realisation that he is amid a group of people dawns within seconds.

"You can't even laugh, can you?" She says.

He shakes his head as if she can see him.

"You know what?" She says.

"Yes."

"I think we shouldn't be friends."

"Why?"

"Because you never fail to get on my nerves. It happens literally every single time we talk," she says, "And unfortunately I like it when people does that. So I should rather ignore you."

"Your loss," Gregor says.

"You're a strange man, Gregor. Very strange. In the morning, you were literally hallucinating in front of me. And when you saw the boss, you were acting as if you were his boss."

"You know what?" Gregor says. "When I looked at him, I thought he was a Santa Claus."

A laugh breaks from the other end. She laughs more than what is necessary and Gregor thinks that she will never stop. Every laughter seems contagious to Gregor, and now he wishes he could laugh like her; laugh the heart out, without noticing anyone around him. "Santa Claus? Yeah," she says, "I heard you saying that shit to me. *Why is Santa Claus here? Is there a celebration today?*"

"Yup," Gregor says and she starts laughing again. He suddenly feels embarrassed---for firstly, she is laughing at his own mental condition, and secondly, he has a sudden feeling that the people who are surrounding him can also hear her. He further turns towards the window, as if to hide his embarrassment from others.

She laughs for probably a whole minute, and then puts a hold to it. "Excuse me, please." She says, and she remains on the call for a few more minutes. All he can hear is the sound of her breath, and some noise from the background. "You know what, when I think about it, he can actually be a Santa Claus. Probably someone should insist that he be Santa Claus this Christmas. That will be the day I laugh myself to death." She says, continuing her laughter.

"I have a strong intuition that today's that day," Gregor says.

"How is it like to live with hallucinations?" She asks out of the blue, her laughter finding a sudden full stop. "Is it scary?"

"It's rather funny, I must say."

"I think hallucinations spring out of traumas right?"

"Traumas? Maybe."

"Hmm," she says. "I heard a buzz about you in the office. I don't know if it is true or not. But I am sure it's traumatic."

"What is it?"

"That you witnessed someone's death."

Gregor is silent.

"Is it true?" She asks.

"Maybe."

"Maybe, maybe. I think your maybe means yes," she says. "Is that what you say when some girl asks whether you love her?"

Gregor starts to say maybe again, so he holds himself back.

"Did I upset you with my questions?"

"Maybe you did. Most of the time, the things that seem funny to you, aren't such for others. Death is not funny"

"Anything is funny when we decide to laugh at it. Sometimes that is what we should do, Gregor. Laugh at the things that keep on haunting you. Just don't take life seriously. It is going to end anyways. Also, you were right when you said that I can't understand human emotions perfectly. That's true. But, I'm working on it too, along with my anger issues," she says and she does not say anything for sometime, as if waiting for a response from Gregor's end. But she does not receive any. "Sorry if I spoiled your day."

My day; my days aren't going well in the first place, for you to spoil it, Gregor thinks and disconnects the call, without a response. After speaking what he did, he feels a lump in his throat, which he finds hard to get rid of. He looks outside the train window, in an attempt to calm himself down, and rather not expose his own emotions before his co-passengers. Without being able to control his tears, he gets up and heads towards the toilet. He stops when he reached the exact spot where he saw the musician for the last time. He opens the train door, and stands there, looking outside as the world moves, welcoming him. Gregor imagines what would have been the final thoughts the musician had in his mind, when he chose his own death. Thoughts are fast and loud; no one knows what all thoughts run through the minds of a person in the fraction of a second. Thoughts are not just fast and loud, but it is also powerful, for it has the power to change everything for better or worse. But, at that moment, Gregor's mind is devoid of any thoughts. When he finally gets the courage to jump out of the train, the train loses its speed; he looks out of the train and realises that the train is now approaching his station. He pulls himself back and sighs; For a moment, he indulges himself in the beauty of breathing. Like someone said, Not today; or rather Not now.

As he looks outside the train, he finds that his vision is blurred due to the tear drops which are inadvertently filling his eyes, almost resisting a fall down. For a moment, he is not feeling any sorrow or any kind of emotion, which makes him wonder where the tear drops come from. All he sees before him are rings of different lights. Red, gold, green, navy blue and some white. Again. This time, he is sure that the Christmas celebrations have started. The speed of the train further declines and it finally comes to a halt. He gets out and looks at the train he has just travelled in. It is exactly the same train he had seen in the morning; the Christmas themed one.

He is confused, and almost for a moment, he forgets that he is hallucinating again. He turns away from the train, and looks for the Santa Claus and he spots one smoking a pipe at a corner of the railway station opposite to him. This time, he knows that he shall not trust his mind, so he walks up to a gentleman who is standing next to him; who has just left out of the same train as Gregor.

"Excuse me, sir," Gregor asks him, and points at the Santa Claus who is making circles of smoke. The man looks at Gregor with a smile on his face; he may be someone who has a perfect job; or rather he does not work at all, which makes Gregor wonders what brings more happiness; is it employment or unemployment? And he comes to a conclusion that neither brings happiness, and happiness is something rather more profound and of a higher status; happiness, no matter what the cause is too divine to define; that is the most suitable definition of happiness. All these thoughts rush through his mind unnoticeable, as if the fog that travels with the wind, and he looks at the man standing in front of him, as if he is a saint.

"Yes, young man," the man says and looks in the direction of Gregor's finger.

"Do you see a Santa Claus there?" Gregor asks.

"Yes. Yeah. I see a Santa Claus."

"And is he smoking?"

"Yes, he is," the man says with the smile on his face widening, as if what Gregor said is the most wholesome thing someone has told him the whole day. "What? Did you think that you were hallucinating?" The man says with a laughter breaking out of him. He laughs briefly, and his body shakes in the mirth. Gregor has never seen such a peaceful laugh in a long time. Although there is nothing funny about the situation, some people always find a reason for a good laugh, even if it is at the expense of others. But, Gregor realises something about himself, that he has more of a sensitive mind to achieve that level of happiness. He tries to remember his face, that is hidden behind the hideous head of an insect; the unhappy, dark face, that is in dire need of the radiance of a smile. For a moment, he thinks that what Meera said was right: sometimes we need to laugh at our own misfortunes, just as how we laugh at those of other people.

Gregor looks at the man, finding what to say in response. His look turns into a stare as he is surprised at how the man had exhumed that word, hallucination, from the depths of his conscience. That's when a phone started ringing; the melody of a song in a movie which is released recently. The man looks at the phone in his hand; that's not the origin of the ringtone. He pulls out another mobile phone from his pocket, only to find that that neither is the phone which is ringing. "Ah, the phone in my backpack," he says, as he opens the bag and fumbles for his third phone. "This is my misfortune, see, how many phones I have to carry. I am even getting confused with the ringtones boy, every single time." He pulls out the mobile from the bag. He looks at the screen and his face changes. "This guy is calling me for the thousandth time. Please hang on. Let me take this call, ok, young man. Trust me, one of us is going to die today!" The man moves away from Gregor, closer to the platform as he takes the call and starts talking. Given the distance, Gregor can still hear the voice of the man, although Gregor does not pay much attention to it. He is clearly shouting at the person on the other end in the lowest of the voice, without letting the other person speak. Gregor, to distract himself, looks at the Santa Claus, who still continues to smoke the pipe. Gregor looks at the whirls of smoke Santa is puffing out, and he loses himself in the art of it. The Santa Claus looks at him for a second, then turns his face back, as if he is not interested.

The man returns after disconnecting the call, which took almost two minutes. Gregor is observing the Santa Claus, and he gets a notion that the Santa Claus is preparing to leave the station.

"You have no idea how stupid these people are... Uhm, what is your name? I forgot to ask," the man says. Gregor although is listening to the man, his concentration rests on the Santa Claus who is still smoking the pipe, showing some signs of leaving the station.

"Gregor. That's my name."

"Gregor? What is your second name?"

"Gregor is alone," Gregor says, his face showing visible distraction.

The man ignores the distraction writ on his face. He doesn't tell his name only because Gregor disn't show the courtesy to ask his name.

"It's strange, lonely names," he says.

"Of course it is."

"Yeah. I was saying, Mr. Gregor, that was a singer who called me for some chance in movies. You have no idea how many times he contacted me. He doesn't interest me, you know? He is quite bad, and thinks he is some Mohammed Rafi."

"Oh, I know someone who sings very well. I met him a few days back," Gregor says, still distracted.

"I actually stopped working with musicians, you know? At least for sometime. After a major incident. These singers can't really take rejection properly," the man says. The man looks at Gregor, examining him from head to toe and especially his hair. "Moreover, I don't want musicians, Gregor. I want you."

Gregor suddenly shifts his attention from the Santa Claus and looks at the man in front of him. Gregor wonders if his eyes and mouth gave out signs of hunger and thirst. "What do you mean?" Gregor asks.

"No. I mean, I think you seem fit to act in movies," the man says. "Do you have any such interests?"

"Movies? Of course not," Gregor says in an inattentive tone. He watches the Santa Cluse and finds that he has started moving. "Anyways, it was nice meeting you, sir. I hope you find your dream actor."

Gregor says and almost runs towards the Santa Claus, who is now moving out of the railway station.

"Hello, Santa," Gregor calls him from behind. The Santa Claus stops and turns back. Gregor thinks he saw a smile forming on the Santa Claus's face. The Santa Claus looks so real, and Gregor stands breath taken for a moment. He feels as if he has seen someone straight from heaven. Gregor smiles at him, but there is no smile on Santa's face.

"What do you want?" Santa asks.

"Where are the other Santas?" Gregor asks.

The Santa looks at him confused, with a huge frown. "What?"

"I just want to know if I am hallucinating."

"Young man, do you need any help?"

"Yeah. Where are the other Santas and the reindeers? I thought I saw them in the morning, along with you."

"Along with me? You are mistaken. I don't remember meeting anyone like me today," Santa says, the frown still hanging on top of his eyes like grand white clouds.

Gregor sighs and stands desolate.

"Can I leave?" The Santa asks.

"Yeah. I am sorry. It is my mistake."

The Santa Claus is not interested in spending more time with a madman. So he turns back and leaves without a farewell smile.

Gregor looks back to see the other man standing at the exact same spot as he had left him. He has his eye on him and it seems that he is examining his movements and making judgements.

"Anything wrong?" The man asks.

Gregor shrugs and starts walking towards the exit.

CHAPTER TWENTY-FIVE

The realisation that the man he had just met may exactly be the man who had caused the death of his one-evening friend dawns on him gradually as he walks through the road that led to his home. Gregor looks around and sees complete darkness. The streetlights are not glowing tonight. Maybe the power is down. Earlier that evening, as he was walking to the railway station from his office, he had seen dark clouds hanging on the sky, threatening a downfall soon. Maybe it is going to rain, and like a quick verification to his thoughts, lightning flashes and thunder roars. He has forgotten to take the umbrella today, and he realises that he could have bought one on his way to the railway station, but his mind was then preoccupied with various thoughts, as it is now. He turns the flashlights on and continues the walk. Fear starts gnawing at him from the fingertips of his left hand and works its way upwards to his elbow, the shoulder, his neck, and then his head. It continues its course of journey throughout his body.

"Do you like to walk in the dark?" Someone had asked him, a few years back, one night in a well-lit cafe.

"I don't know. I haven't tried it yet."

"Even I haven't. But I would like to try it, atleast once."

"I do think I will enjoy it," Gregor said, faking courage.

"No way. I really don't know. I don't even know what I should expect! I admit I am afraid to try it, in the first place. But I believe we should try everything that we are afraid of."

Gregor looked at his cup of coffee and took a sip.

"Maybe we should try it tonight."

"But, in a city that never sleeps, night feels like day," Gregor said.

"You are right. Also, we are two. How the hell can we experience a dark night alone!" That person laughed.

It still reverberates in his head.

A drop falls on the centre of his head, as if an assertion. The rain drops increase in number very fast, and Gregor gathers his hat from his bag and puts it on. It has already become a heavy rain. Gregor attempts to run towards his house. It is barely a few hundred metres away. But then he stops.

He sees multiple flashes of light approaching him from a distance. Along with the light, he hears the galloping of a few animals. He also hears the hoots of old men. He thinks that it may be the Santa Clauses and the reindeers he saw in the morning. They move so fast and have already reached near him, which gives him no space to run towards the side of the road, so that he can allow them to pass by. They did not slow down either. They crash into Gregor, and he falls down, his face first. The reindeers now run over him, and he cries in pain. It was over in a few seconds. Gregor tries to get up, but with pain, he continues to lay there. His legs and his forehead seem to hurt.

"Ah! I think it's those bastards again!" Someone says, rushing towards Gregor.

"I think they hit a man this time."

He opens his eyes and sees two pairs of legs, standing nearby him. There are moments when you open your eyes as if from a dream, only to realise that you are not actually in a dream, but in fact living, breathing, and physically present; there are moments when living does not feels like living, but rather like a dream, and all of a sudden you wake up into a different life.

Even when he is in pain, and is unaware of what just happened, the only thought that runs through his mind is the fact that he has to be present at the office tomorrow, or else his job will be at stake.

Two men pull him up, so that he can now stand on his legs.

"Do you feel pain in your legs?"

"Yes, on my ankles. But I can stand without help."

"That's ok," the man says. "Tell us where do you live."

Although he lives closer, these men do not know him, or else they cannot identify him because it is dark. But either way, he rarely gets out of his house, except for work, and it is rather plausible that these men do not know him.

Gregor tells the directions.

"Do you want to go to the house, or to a hospital? If you want, I can take you to the hospital nearby," the man offers.

"Maybe to the hospital; to get the wounds dressed," Gregor says.

"Ok, let me return with my bike. There is no use complaining about those boys. Better ignore them. Who knows whether they will come to our house and slit our throats?"

Gregor nods.

The man goes across the road.

Gregor stands in the rain, shivering, with the other man who has joined them. It is two weeks ago when it rained for the last time, and now it pours like it is lashing down the miseries it has scraped together in the past couple of weeks.

Tragicomedy

CHAPTER TWENTY-SIX

In the summer of 1999, when most parts of the world were scorching under unprecedented levels of heat, it rained continuously at Gregor's town for weeks. The rain's harsh tenure seemed to have no end so Gregor's father had to cancel all the vacation plans he had previously made, forcing Gregor to stay at home and read books. Although he felt disappointed with it, what affected him more was that his father was always hovering around him, watching him, asking him questions out of boredom; questions from the books he was reading; questions about his studies; and school. When Gregor used to engage in other activities like scribbling something, drawing something, trying his hands on carpentry, or simply passing the time like watching the rain, his father used to discourage him, making sure that Gregor only read books. His father believed that great things came only to those who excelled academically. One thing that relaxed Gregor was that his father was not so furious during vacations; that he was not beaten or scolded at. Gregor felt happy with whatever kind of freedom he got because any kind of freedom was better than servitude. He also tried not to upset his father and spent most of his time sitting down on his hard plastic chair, reading each of the books his father had collected over time in the home library, and putting up with the questions and lectures of his father, whenever those came forth.

Another phenomenon that came with the heavy rains was the appearance of bugs and other insects, the uninvited guests who tenured for free. Bugs were everywhere, on the floor, on the walls, on the ceiling, on the bed, climbing up through his limbs, taking flight and landing on his hair. Gregor almost ignored their existence. Although insects were there wherever he looked, he saw through them as if they were invisible. He just randomly brushed them away or plucked them off without hurting them, because he rather used to consider them as his friends. When one or two bugs used to come near him and seek his attention, he used to observe them and talk to them. He would be distracted by their presence for a good three or four minutes and used to gracefully go back to his book, and think about the need to finish them so that he can start with the next book. On a few occasions when his father would go out in the beating rain to finish some work, Gregor used to turn the lights off and sleep. Thanks to the rain, it was always dark inside his room, no matter what time it was. When his father arrives, he jumps up from the bed, turns the light on, lands himself on the chair, opens the book, and pretends to continue reading the book. With the brightness of the light inside and the darkness outside, the purple walls around him found a level of depth that was rather haunting. His father was so adamant that Gregor should stay in his room with his books, and not do anything else. He even prevented Gregor from spending much time with his baby sister, who was only a few months old. Gregor's father used to give him that kind of glance which made Gregor feel bad about himself. "You should not waste even a second of your life," his father used to say. "The second you wait, someone better will fly past you. Always keep this in mind." Although he felt uneasy at first, after some time, he started getting adapted to the kind of stagnant lifestyle he was leading; he rather started enjoying it, more than anything else.

One such day, while he was on his chair, reading a book about a scientist and his inventions, his father appeared by the door. His piercing eyes were on the floor.

"Ah! These dirty bugs!" He exclaimed.

That was when Gregor looked down. He saw a few number of bugs moving towards all directions.

"Are you breeding these or what?"

Gregor looked at his father with big eyes. Despite his reading, his brain was so underformed, that he did not know what to say.

"It's all because of your lack of hygiene!"

Gregor was still unaware of what he must say. He looked as if he was studying his father's face which was changing hues, from disgust to anger, seeing the swarm of bugs.

"The problem with these bugs is that even if we kill few of them, they will still come back in a larger number. And, it's only in your room!"

Gregor continued to look at his father, wishing that he also had something to say, but his mouth and brain seemed to have been shut down.

"Don't touch them. Also, if you inadvertently allow it to climb on your body, then it will secretly drink your blood, and may even go into your ears."

His father warned him, looked at the bugs for one last time, then left the room, went back to his own room, and started reading his magazines, which Gregor had no access to. His father never talked about the bugs later.

Gregor shut the book and placed it on the table. What his father said, continued to stay in his mind. So after that, he did not take his eyes off any of the bugs which were present in the room. He studied their movements and wondered which one of them was coming his way, which one was going away, and which one would potentially climb on his body and walk up to his head. Gregor started feeling the movement of bugs throughout his body; through his hair, his arms, his shoulders, his neck, his chest, his abdomen, his thighs, and his legs, and he continued to brush away imaginary bugs off his body. He even started shutting the door and examining his named body in private to see if there were any bugs. But, he could not find any. He did not know if he should have felt disappointed with it.

Although it was raining heavily that night, he found it difficult to sleep, as he kept on imagining bugs moving through his body, and sliding their way into his ears. He used to get up in the middle of the night, to examine his bed sheets for the presence of bugs. He brushed off imaginary bugs and returned to his bed and attempted to sleep. Later, even after it stopped raining, the bugs would not leave him at peace; they continued to walk through his back, his legs, and his torso, even when he was elsewhere.

CHAPTER TWENTY-SEVEN

Gregor opens his eyes and continues to hear the sound of the rain. It fills his ears, envelops him, and he feels rather peaceful, contrary to the kind of dreams he had last night. Last night, Gregor dreamt of himself as a boy, the kind of nightmare he hadn't had in a very long time, or rather such dreams might have been a part of the multitude of dreams that he saw every night, just that he did not remember them upon waking up. But today, as he wakes up from sleep, it is the only thing that remains in his head, and for a moment, those fears he had as a child, seem to return.

He dreamt he was sleeping soundly in a room that was rather bright with shady lights on. He was lying on a bed at the centre of the room, which made him rather claustrophobic, and sometime into the night, a bug started climbing up through his legs and found its way straight up to his ears. It entered, and made holes through his skull as if building a tunnel that led up to his brain. And he woke up suddenly when the bug started devouring the folds of his intellect. He remembered himself being in his old house, and the one thing that continues to stay in his mind is that purple wall which felt more emphasized and brighter when it was dark outside and the bright light inside.

The first thing Gregor does upon waking up is look at the wall, and confirm that it isn't purple, but a shade of lighter green, which does not get emphasized in the dark. Gregor heaves a sigh of relief, and he feels rather comfortable and safe. It was Gregor who had bought their new home, and now Gregor feels rather proud of himself, despite the beating headache, for having created an environment that did not cause him fear or insecurity.

He continues to stay like that in bed for a few more minutes. It seems that he was still in those days where rain was a sign of holiday and laziness was affordable. He closes his eyes to invite sleep again, but he opens it immediately as reality strikes him. To confirm, he checks his mobile phone to find that it is just Friday and he has to wait for another day to pass, so that he can finally afford this safety and comfort. Besides...

Besides... Besides... Today is that big event that his boss has been hyping up for the past few days. He should be there in the office on time. He knows that no excuses will work today. Gregor struggles to get up from the bed, but he cannot. He feels pain throughout his body, especially his ankles. He doesn't want to look at his body, because he knows that he will not be able to see his wounds.

It is with the striking pain that he remembers the accident which had happened last night. Someone had picked him up from the road and had taken him to the hospital. The doctor had said there were multiple injuries, especially on his torso, knees and ankles. The wounds weren't complicated, so they were dressed and the stranger had taken him back to his house. He even helped Gregor into the house, and had explained the situation to his parents and sister.

The parents of course knew who this "stranger" was, although Gregor was seeing him for the first time. Now he realises that he does not even remember the face of the man, so that he can pass a smile or thank him later. Two constant things Gregor remembers of last night are the excruciating pain and the never-ending storm, and probably... and probably how they asked him to lay on the hospital cot, how there was a mirror right in front of the cot, and he saw his reflection clearly in it; how he had not seen him but a huge miserable bug who can't even handle the little pain that life has offered; the nurses tried their best with force and words to calm the bug, to get it settled and start treating.

After a few more seconds of contemplation, with rain in the backdrop, he tries to get up again but feels as if some kind of weight is pulling him down, which denies him any kind of motion. Also, with every action, he inadvertently pulls at some of his wounds, which makes him groan, but those groans are so silent, as if not to invite any kind of attention from the other inhabitants of his house. He does not want to call them and ask for help, thereby appearing miserable and weak.

When he skilfully lifts his torso off the bed, he finds that his vision is blurred; he sees his body, the body of an ugly insect, as two. He finally succeeds in lifting his torso completely off the bed. He moves backwards and leans on the headboard. He looks at his limbs and tries to look past the insect's skin, but to his disappointment, he is not able to see anything besides that. But his right ankle hurts so badly, he feels as if his wounds, especially that on his ankle, are infected by a grumble of maggots. He realises that he will not even be able to set his foot on the floor, let alone get up and walk. He remains like that, leaning on the headboard, dejected, slowly accepting his fate. He finds himself surrounded by a symphony of emotions, cut in by the music of the rain. If possible, he needs to be present at the office in two hours, or else, he shall call his boss now, explain the situation to him, and take leave. He wants to decide, and the choice is rather obvious.

His phone rings. He finds the name, Meera, as he had saved it yesterday.

"Hey, good morning," she says from the other end.

"Yes, good morning. What's up?"

"Just wanted to say sorry to you. I just called to make things up between us. And last night, I promised myself that it'll be the first thing I do tomorrow."

"No. You don't have to be apologetic for who you are. I understand it... I understand it these days," he says.

"Yeah. I am never apologetic and I rarely say sorry to anyone. I have only used that word a handful of times in my life, which makes that word a special one to me. But I realise I was a bit over the top yesterday, and I must say that you are probably the nicest person I've ever met. So you deserve it."

"Trust me, I'm cool," he says. *I have a million other things to think about*, he wants to add, but he does not.

"All the best for today," she says. "Impress that fucking whale."

Gregor cringes at hearing an abusive word, first thing in the morning.

"I guess, I need to wait for that," Gregor says.

"Why?"

"I'm not going to the office today."

"What? Given the workaholic you are, I imagine you in a hospital, dying. I mean why else wouldn't you come?"

"Last night, I met with an accident, and I am not even able to stand up properly."

"So, you sure are dying. See, I was right about that."

"I wish I was."

"What?"

"I wish I was dying, and was actually dead by now."

"You wanna die while talking to me? You really want to get me into trouble, don't you? But, yes, people do die while talking to me, metaphorically." She starts a laugh and stops it abruptly. "I don't know how many more times I'll have to say sorry today, but I really am. You are there dying, and I was about to laugh my guts out."

"I can understand what you meant by the metaphorical death. I'm feeling it, right now."

"No way. Don't be. That was not the first thing I wanted to do today."

Gregor is silent. She has also gone silent on her part, and all he hears now is the noise of the rain. Then, to his surprise, laughter rises from her side.

"I'm a tragedy. A real one," she says.

"You're a tragicomedy, a real one."

"Ok, I get what you are trying to say. Alright," She says. Both are silent for some time, then she talks again. "Don't get the wrong meaning when I say this, but imagine us getting married. Our marriage will be much more catastrophic than Dr. Oppenheimer's nuke."

"I get the gist of what you are trying to say," he says. "But who in the world is this Oppenheimer?"

"Take some spare time off your work and read some history. He is definitely an unforgettable genius. As unforgettable to the Japanese as me to you."

"That clearly explains who he was and what he did to the people of Japan! That was a clear analogy."

"Yeah. I think Nolan is going to make a movie about him. If you don't want to read history, just wait for the movie. Or... just... just simply read the history. A history book is less tedious than a Nolan movie."

"Damn! I don't even remember the last movie I watched."

"Dude, what do you even do with your life?"

"Probably, live and die for my family."

"And top your name in the family history, maybe. A martyr."

"A martyr. Yes, that is what I am going to be."

"Dude just found his goal in life! Congrats!" She says. "Do you know who else is more terrifying than me and Dr. Oppenheimer? Our boss, the clown, the whale I was talking about. Did you call him to inform leave?"

"I was trying to make a decision. Whether to get some rest or come to work."

"I get the feeling like you are dying. Otherwise, why would you even consider taking a leave on this exact day? You must have gone nuts. And if you are calling the boss, please don't wait even a second. Every moment that passes is like a ticking time bomb. Call him as soon as possible. He will get mad at you. But, I think you have no choice."

"I get a feeling that my job is going to be at stake."

"No, no. Just remain confident and give him a call, explain your situation and listen to whatever he says. He is a human after all. I'm sure he'll understand you."

Gregor knows that even Meera does not believe what she just said.

"Yeah." He sighs.

"Just fucking eat that frog."

"Just fucking eat that what?"

"Never mind. Forget what I just said, and give that call without any delay. So now, cut the call and call that whale. Imagine him answering from under the ocean," she says and laughs longer than what is required. Gregor does not laugh, due to the million thoughts that have started growing inside his mind, like viruses. "Bye, dude. Explain it to him, and tell me how it goes."

"Ok. Sure," Gregor says and cuts the call. That's when he sees his mother who has by then appeared by the door. She smiles at him, and he returns it.

"How's your head? Does it still hurt?" she asks innocently, unknowingly sending a surge of pain through his body.

"What?" Gregor's face contorts in horror as a sudden, sharp pain explodes from the centre of his skull. It spreads rapidly, like fire through dry leaves, igniting his entire nervous system with unbearable agony. He clutches both sides of his head, pressing hard as if he can crush the pain into submission.

His mother rushes to his side, sits beside him and places her hands on his trembling shoulders, trying in vain to soothe him.

"It's killing me," Gregor gasps, his voice strained with desperation. "It's like my head's on fire. I can't bear it."

"You seemed fine only a minute ago," she says, her voice filled with concern. "What's happening, Gregor?"

Gregor groans as the pain intensifies, spreading to his eyes, and making them throb painfully. "I didn't even know there was anything wrong with my head," he mutters, barely able to speak. "The pain started the moment you asked about it."

"You bought home painkillers yesterday," his mother says softly. "You can take one after breakfast. But first, go freshen up. You'll feel better once you've had some medicine."

As she speaks, Gregor's mind drifts back to his conversation with Meera. How pleasant it was, how comforting her jokes and the sound of her laughs were, although it didn't fail to cringe or offend him. He could still hear the rain in the background, mingling with her laughter. But now, it feels like life has turned on him in an instant, dragging him from the warmth of that moment into the searing pain he is in now.

His mother wipes away her tears, trying to comfort him. "Gregor, please, get up. Then you can take the medicine, and I promise you'll feel better." She gently tugs at his elbow, urging him to move.

Gregor's fists are pressed against the sides of his head. "It's... not getting better," he mutters.

"Come on, let me help you out of bed," she offers, leaning in closer.

"I can do it myself," Gregor snaps, pushing her away gently. He tries to move his legs, but it feels like his right one is made of lead; as if it has swollen or some weight is holding it down. He struggles, but the leg refuses to budge. Frustration bubbles up inside him, and he turns to his mother. "Can you please just leave me alone and let me handle this myself?"

She pauses, uncertainty flickering across her face.

"I just feel so miserable," he continues, his voice breaking, "When I can't even lift my leg with you watching."

For a moment, she just looks at him, torn between wanting to help and respecting his wish for solitude. Finally, she wipes her tears, rises from the bed, and quietly leaves the room.

Gregor gets the phone from his bed and dials his boss, who attends the call within a few rings. The promptness with which the boss attends the call makes him stammer when he greets him good morning.

"Good morning. Haven't you left already?" He says in response.

"Sir, last night, I met with an accident. I have some minor injuries on my body, especially on my leg and head, so I am not in a condition to come to the office today. Sorry sir, but I will be absent today."

There is silence on his end, and Gregor finds it odd. Still, he waits for his boss to respond.

"Okay, take rest," he says finally, as if saying something exactly opposite to what he has in his mind. His voice has clear changes from how he talked at first.

"I am sorry, sir."

"Yeah. It's okay." He says and disconnects the call.

Gregor stares back at his phone screen, without knowing what to do. He then thinks of calling Meera, and that is when he receives a call from her.

"Man, I am sorry. I must confess that I was spying on you. I just saw that you called someone. Was it that pervert Manu? What did he say?"

"I explained the situation to him, and he responded it with Okay, take rest."

"What? No way. You must have called the wrong person."

"No, it's the same person; I even checked it while I was talking to him. I had the same doubt."

"Definitely. Because he is not so gentle."

"He is not, but he has to be. Also, it's only morning, and maybe he doesn't want to spoil his day, by getting mad at me."

"That explains. I think he has a kind of toxic positivity. Don't you think so?"

"I have never had such observations, to be honest."

"To be honest, do you even know what toxic positivity means?"

"I can guess what that is."

"Pathetic," she says. "Toxic positivity. That's something only rich people can afford."

"I will afford it someday then."

"Dude, you are going to be a martyr. Toxic positivity is too big of an aspiration for you. You can't even attain a percentage of that, with the kind of work you do. I don't mean to say that you work badly. But, you work for someone else, not for yourself, and that is not the real way to earn some real money. You got me?"

"But, you do the same," Gregor says.

"I don't aspire to have toxic positivity. Besides, this is more than what I can ask from life, and I am cool with it."

"But you work for Manu, and that is a humiliation," Gregor says.

"It is a humiliation I am rather okay with. I don't think we can all ask for a perfect life, can we?"

"Everyone has a heavy load of advice when it's concerning the lives of others," Gregor says.

"No, I don't find anything wrong with how I am talking to you. I now find myself at my wisest level."

Then they find themselves at an inevitable moment of silence. The rain still continues in full volume.

"I don't know where that headache went away," Gregor says.

"Headache?"

"Yeah. I remember having a headache right before I called you. But now it's gone."

"Man, listen." She pauses and then continues to talk. "I might sound like a balm now, but what I really am is a fucking storm; a storm that no one can handle." She says then pauses. "But, I must say that it's refreshing to know that something good still remains within me, although I'm sure it's nothing but a prank I play on myself."

"Ah! And now the headache starts again. Thank you very much."

"See? That's what I actually am, and you misunderstood me for a balm; you are welcome," she says, breaking into a laugh.

"I may cut the call. I guess the headache is getting severe," Gregor says, stammering and groaning.

"Man, I think you got into some serious trouble yesterday. Do you have a head injury, or what?" She asks. He tries to bear with her at least for some more time. He holds the phone tighter, as if it may fall from his hand any moment. For some reason, he does not want to hang up on her.

"It seems so."

"It seems so?"

"Yes. When I touched my head, I felt bandages."

"Aren't you even sure about what's happening to your body?"

Gregor shrugs as if she can see him.

"Please cut the call and take some rest. Ah! It's raining and I don't even want to-"

Gregor hangs up the call, before letting her finish articulating her thoughts. The phone slips out of his hand, and lands face down, with a dull thud. But he doesn't reach for it; instead, he collapses sideways onto the bed. For someone who can see him as he sees himself, they may see but a crushed wasp trampled under someone's harsh boots and then electrocuted by a mosquito bat. The pain in his head is so intense that it drowns out every other ache in his body. His mind starts a chant and tells him that today is the day he is going to die—a thought that seems exaggerated given his condition, but the mind has a way of amplifying fears, distorting them until they overshadow reality. Despite the cold, rain-lashed weather, sweat beads on his skin. His body trembles uncontrollably and tears spill from the corners of his eyes. The only word that escapes his lips is a desperate plea for the woman he has pushed away just moments before.

"Mother! Mother!"

CHAPTER TWENTY-EIGHT

Although Gregor is on leave, he still has got work to do from home.

"We need to bring together as many people as we can. Nothing is enough in a big program like this," his colleagues say.

Gregor does not make any excuse or complaint, as he had already been given enough liberties like allowing him to be at home. When he is resting, he keeps the phone closer to his side, keeping the volume up, so that he can be vigilant when someone from work needs his assistance. Although he is not in a right state, physically and mentally, he still gives his best. His phone has no rest, calls arrive one after another till the program gets over. The program ends at seven in the evening, and his colleague at work calls him to brief about the program.

"The program was not a success as we had envisioned," he says. "I felt like we could have done a lot more, but there was a lack of manpower. It's so hard to explain. We tried our best. Our boss even appointed a few people on contract basis, but even then we couldn't do it perfectly. For me, it was heartbreaking in the end. I guess it is the same for everyone else. Boss is not happy either."

Although Gregor knows that it is irrational, he can't shake the feeling that everything went wrong because of his absence. He knows deep down it's not his fault, but he's certain his boss will try to pin the blame on him. Even so, Gregor finds a strange sense of pride in the idea that he's indispensable at the office, that without him, nothing works as it should. It's a comforting thought, although it lacks any real substance or practicality. But what haunts him more is the fact that no matter how hard he tries, he always ends up disappointing himself and others. When the moment of judgment comes, he feels like nothing more than a failure, marked in glaring red.

CHAPTER TWENTY-NINE

Gregor has never been a bright student in school. When his results of seventh standard came out, it was revealed that he had failed in one subject. His father concluding that Gregor needed more discipline, decided to send him to a boarding school far away, believing it would help him perform better in school and in life. One such day, while Gregor was away at the boarding school, his cousin visited his house with family. She was a year older than him, and only had a faint memory of a summer vacation where they used to play all sorts of games, before she moved to a different place with her family. All she remembered of him was how they both felt to be similar in thoughts and interests. But she, ignorant about worldly affairs as she is, came to his house in hopes that she will be able to see him again. That day, when she walked up to his room, and opened the door, a butterfly flew down to her face, startling her. With a mix of surprise and innocence, she exclaimed to everyone present, "I thought Gregor turned into a butterfly!"

Maybe due to the restricting nature of his hostel life, or the bullying and ragging of his seniors and peers, or the daunting isolation that he faced there, Gregor could not perform well in his studies. Besides that, he started falling sick every other day. There were times when he took leave from school for a whole week, but the hostel staff did not take the struggle of calling his parents and informing him. One day, almost a year had passed, his parents and sister made a visit to his school, without notice. They came to know that Gregor was absent that day. Then they headed straight to the hostel. There was no trace of him outside the building and the hostel staff was not useful when it came to providing information.

So they went straight to his room and knocked on it. There was no answer. They found that the door was not locked. So they pushed it open. What they saw in the room got them terrified. Gregor was alone in the room. He was in the bed, facing away from the door. He only had a boxer on. He was shivering, and they found the fan to be rotating at full speed. His body was unlike what they had seen as they watched him leave. He has turned into nothing but skin and bones. When his mother went forward and asked him to turn towards them, he obeyed, and what they saw was a face that was devoid of life.

They did not waste a moment for thought and brought him back home. Since then, for a few years that passed, his mother rarely left his side. He was sent to a local school. His parents took proper measures to ensure that he did not face any mistreatments, although he had to face some seemingly harmless bullying that he could not complain to anyone of. He also did not want to be the one in the group who spoils the fun, when his friends laughed at his body. He realised that if he needed friends, he might also have to stay deaf and blind to some silent bullying. He realised that most friendships are nothing but a combination of love and bullying. He realised it was normal, although sometimes he found it difficult to bear with those torments. Although Gregor did feel targeted at times, he did not react in any way or shared it with anyone. But as a result of these silent and loud lots of laughter, Gregor started hating his body and even stopped looking at himself in the mirror.

CHAPTER THIRTY

Maybe a day has passed. Maybe it is more than a day. Maybe it is just a few hours. When Gregor opens his eyes, he sees as if in a dream, a face that is familiar yet forgotten; a face which takes him on a course down the memory lane, where they used to live in the same house, eat the same food, play the same game. Gregor does not remember much about his childhood; for that matter, he does not even remember events from his recent past. Gregor has this habit of burning down the bridges he has crossed, so that he will never cross them again. He automatically forgets his memories, no matter how good or bad they are. But there still remains some residues in the end, and they will try to gain life at some specific moments in his life. It is one such moment. His cousin was probably his only friend in his childhood. She is barely two years older than him; loving, playful and enthusiastic. Although Gregor has forgotten everything else, he still remembers the pain he felt when she left his home to somewhere far, like she might never return again. Gregor has never seen her hence. Gregor has heard of her marriage, which he couldn't attend, and her childbirth, a girl or boy, and he does not know anything else about her, other than the fact that she is still alive.

As Gregor looks at her, those residues within him gets triggered, and it reflects in his face, as a bright smile. He thinks that he is dreaming for a second; he also wants to ask the same question to her, but he simply refrains, and continues to smile at her. He tries to sit straight in his bed; he is too drowsy to attempt that, but with her help, he sits straight and looks at her.

"What day is it?" Gregor asks.

She looks at him with a smile that gives off embarrassment. "You're seeing me after 20-22 years, and that is the first thing you got to ask me?" Her smile widens. Gregor's face suddenly reflects the embarrassment in her face.

"I am sorry," he says. "You came with your husband and child?"

"No, I came alone. They have their own things to do. I was in town, and when I heard about your accident, I just thought of making a visit."

"Trust me. It is nothing big. Just little wounds here and there, you know?"

"What about your office?" She asks.

"I have asked for leave for two days."

"Oh, and tomorrow is a Sunday too, maybe you can get some rest."

He shakes his head. "I don't have Sundays. I mean it's there. And it is a holiday. But a Sunday is too little compared to the rest of the week, and I think it is insignificant."

"Ah, I wish there were five Sundays in a week too. Atleast two or three will do. God should've rested a bit longer after he created the world." She laughs. "But, jokes apart, they say we must enjoy the work we do. So, if the work is too much for you, then you can quit it and find a different one." She taps on his arm.

"Impossible," he laughs. "Tell my mother the same thing and she will throw you out this second. If I lose this job, then I am insignificant too, just like my Sundays. I feel safe with this job, although it's a bit difficult—I mean the job isn't difficult as it is, but it's the work pressure and all. So, I can't take the risk of leaving this job and searching for another one. I think you understand me."

She nods.

"Last time when I came to see you, I thought you had turned into a butterfly," she says, breaking into a brief laughter.

"My mother told me that story. Yeah, it's funny."

"Yeah it's funny. Because butterflies are beautiful, you aren't. Look at you, you have grown uglier," she says with a playful smile, although Gregor finds it difficult to smile at it, the smile she caused in his face started fading. "I expected this time to open the door and find a cockroach, and here it is." She points at him and smiles.

Gregor tries to smile at the joke too, but no matter how hard he tries, his lips resist to go up. His face looks as if he is going to cry. To validate that fact, his eyes start welling up. His cousin looks at him surprised. She rubs his arm, in an attempt to calm him down. "What happened? I was just trying to make a joke."

"I know. I am very well aware of it," he says, wiping the drops of embarrassment off.

"It doesn't seem so," she says. "Why are you crying? You want me out?"

"It's ok. I am sorry for that."

She is silent then. He does not say anything either.

"I didn't mean anything," she says.

"I know."

"Is it difficult for you to control your emotions?"

Gregor sniffles. His eyes are red in colour. He wants her out, but he also wants her to stay. "Sometimes, yes," he says. "See, you didn't even say anything to me, and I almost started crying."

"I have been there too. Have you ever thought of seeing a counsellor? They can really help you, you know?"

Gregor is silent. He just looks at her with a face which is devoid of any emotions. Without knowing what else to do, he nods.

"Think about it and tell me. I will give you a number."

"I don't even have your number." He smiles at her. She returns it.

"Remember how happy we were, back then?"

"I wasn't happy," Gregor shakes his head. "I still am not."

"You know what the secret to happiness is?" She looks at him.

Gregor shakes his head again. "I don't think there's one little secret to happiness. It's complicated."

"It's not complicated. Happiness is the easiest thing there is."

"That's a big statement."

"It's not. Happiness is not big and complicated. It's rather simple and small," she says. "Do you remember how easily I made you cry just moments back? It's that easy to be happy, too." She pauses in an attempt to generate curiousity, although Gregor does not seem curious. "So, do you know what the secret to happiness is?"

"No."

"What do people do when they are happy?" She asks.

"Dance maybe," he says. She retributes him with a slap on his leg.

"They smile," she says. "And that's the secret to happiness. A single and cliched word. Smile. People smile when they are happy, people become happy when they smile. It's interconnected. Smile for yourself, smile for others. That's a small but valuable gift."

Some thought, which is unusual in his thinking, dawns within him. But he smiles. "Which self-help book are you reading right now?"

She retributes him harder than before. "It's not from any self-help book. Consider that as my wisdom from meditating for years."

"Do you meditate?"

"Yes. But, not like a sage; sitting on the floor, closing your eyes and your fingers in some mudras. Sometimes, it's done simply by looking outside the window and watching nature. It's as simple as that."

"If that's the case, I meditate every time."

"You sure do," she says. "I can't wait to hear what wisdom you got."

"If you ask me, I would say that, something as simple as a smile is an answer only to a few things, you know? A very few things. Proper happiness is difficult. It is like a reward for the work we do. I go to work everyday, I give my very best and I am happy how my family is faring because of it. But, I'm unsure of what exactly am I doing with my life. If you think about it, I do nothing that ensures real happiness. Although it may seem meaningful from the outside, it's quite meaningless. It makes me happy, but it doesn't."

"You simply find reasons to undermine the power of your smile," she says. "There's some problem with your thinking if you say that happiness is a reward. It's not. Happiness is within all of us.

Just that we inadvertently set limits to it. We determine what is considered as happiness and what isn't. Due to those limitations we set, it's rather easy for us to define sadness, and that way, it's easier to stay unhappy. There's no need to rely on something external when you have a smile on your face. We expect that person, that object, that drug, that liquor, that work, that experience, to make us happy. Ofcourse, they make you happy, but that happiness is temporary, and this fleeting nature of it can only make you even more desperate. But, think about it. Even when everything else leaves you, you will still have your smile, safe with you. Use it often, or you will forget how to smile."

"It's still difficult for me to simply smile, at times. Even if I do, all I feel is a twitch on my face muscles. Nothing inwards. Maybe I have deprived myself of the power of my smile."

"It's not only you. Sometimes it's difficult for all of us, and it's ok. Real happiness is when we realise that sadness is also a part of life and we shouldn't be pushing it away. We need something negative to appreciate the positive. Just see it that way," she says. Then there's a pause for five whole sections. "But when did our talks become so philosophical?"

Gregor smiles. "We can't always talk about caterpillars and dinosaurs."

"Talking about it, I was really happy back then; with you. Maybe it was my age and naivety. I don't mean to say I'm not happy now. I am happy. But now, it just doesn't feel so pure as it used to be. When I left you and our home, I didn't realise that I was leaving behind my happy childhood too."

"But you never thought about me, or even tried to contact me after that, except for that apparent visit you gave me."

"You didn't try to contact me, either," she retorts. "I thought I didn't matter to you anymore."

"Well, it might be appropriate to say that you didn't matter to me... until now." he says. "We realise it late sometimes, how much we miss some people."

"I think it's great to hear that you miss me." She nods. "I don't know how often I can be with you or whether I can stay in touch. But I'll try; that'a all I can promise."

"That's great, then," Gregor says. "I hope that you stay in touch."

"I'll definitely try. I rarely have free time like this."

"It's ok," he says. "The best thing is, you didn't forget me."

"Who in the world forgets their childhood?"

"Me," he says. "Past is a chasm for me and right now, I'm standing at the edge of it, trying to walk away. There's no doubt that after you leave, I'll start wondering whether your visit was real, or a fragment from a long forgotten dream, movie or rather a book, because when I look back, I only see the chasm."

"I wish I could say the same," she says. "I remember every bit of my past."

"That's a tragedy...?" Gregor says as if he is confused whether to make it a statement or a question.

"It's not. On the fair side, it actually helps me understand things better."

Gregor nods. "I think the problem is mine, then. The burning of bridges."

"Nah, you're good." She winks and smiles. "Everyone has a different method to cope."

CHAPTER THIRTY-ONE

In the evening, Meera calls him to ask for directions to his house. He tries his best to prevent her from coming, since he is not in a mentality to entertain another guest. But she does not listen to his talks and insists on giving her the address. Gregor tells it to her only to make her stop talking. But, she starts calling him every other minute to ask for which turn to take. Gregor waits by the door, leaving everything else behind. It is almost seven in the evening when the calling bell rings. Since it is difficult to get to the door, his sister opens it. He sits there expecting Meera in, already preparing in his mind what to talk and what not to. But, it is not jut one person who comes in. It is atleast five people. Of the five, three of the people are familiar faces in the office; two men, and a woman, whom he has never talked to in his life. Among the other two people, one is Meera, and the other is his boss. That is clearly unexpected and it shocks him. He almost gets up from his chair, to show respect, but his boss asks him to sit down, with a smile. Soon, they all settle down here and there. His boss sits closer to him. Gregor's mother loses all her control on seeing his boss, and she rushes about, and then into the kitchen to treat them with mango shakes. She soon brings it to the table. The boss is the only one who thanks her, and he does that with a gracious smile. For chatterbox like Meera, she is the most silent among the lot that day. Of the three other familiar faces, two of them are the only romantic couple in the office. After asking about Gregor and his health, they start talking to themselves. They even start making laughing sounds, and giggles, making Gregor's father and mother send side glances towards them. Yes, they can be more civil. Gregor cringes at it, and does not look in that way. The other man, without knowing what else to do, talks some nonsense with Meera, and Gregor finds a silent Meera throughout the conversation. It is the boss who asks him the most questions. He wants to know what exactly happened that night. He asks every detail, and even suggests that Gregor may complain about those teenagers to the police, to which Gregor responds, "It is better not to have a conflict with them." The boss nods and then asks in detail about the injuries in his head and on his legs, to which Gregor gives satisfactory answers.

"You know the story of my brother?" The boss asks, and invites the attention of everyone in that room. "My brother was so afraid of exams. He was a bright student, but you know bright students are the ones who are most afraid of exams. He prepared so well for it. But he still had this exam fear and stress, that he will not be able to perform well, that most probably he will fail. But, these are just baseless anxieties, but he believed them. He was convinced that if he wrote the exam, he would fail. Do you know what he did on the day of his exams?" He asks, and everyone in the room, including Gregor's father, shakes their head, feigning interest. But Gregor, suspecting what he is trying to say, sits with an embarrassing smile on his face. Although the story is about his brother, the boss is undoubtedly talking about Gregor. "He intentionally met with an accident. He crashed his bicycle somewhere and returned home with a fractured hand, scratches all over his body and a damaged bicycle, because of which, he couldn't attend the exam that day. Nothing. Gregor's accident just reminded me of this story." Thus his boss succeeds in conveying his baseless and meaningless doubt that Gregor intentionally created the accident to skip the promotional event, and also in making the already awkward situation at home, more awkward. When his boss has finished with the story, Gregor tries to act cool, as if the boss has casually shared an incident from his childhood. He also watches with disgust, the calm smile on his face, as if he is some spiritual Guru who has just shared an insightful anecdote.

CHAPTER THIRTY-TWO

There is a long stretch of silence after the group from the office left. Everyone at home wants to speak out their mind and express their rage, but they all keep quiet. As the silence starts growing more awkward, they all break it and go back to their usual businesses; father and mother to the kitchen and his sister to her study room. They tell what they have in their mind through their strides, closing of doors, and the handling of kitchen tools. Gregor finds himself seated, hurt and overwhelmed. He feels the anxiety rising up within him, but somehow he snaps out of it. Then, without letting his thoughts, which are seeds, grow into a huge tree, he also gets up from the hall, and staggers into his room.

Even when he is in the room, there's nothing much he has to do, which makes the thoughts within him threaten to grow and take root.

For a moment he feels distraught, as if he is nothing but a heavy bunch of mass that is unnecessarily taking up space. His life seems hollow yet suffocating. The fact that he has nothing else to do besides his work terrifies him. He doesn't know what he will do if one day he is kicked out of his office. He knows he will never leave voluntarily. He will cling on as long as possible, like an insect, as long as it can. But what if one day; some reason? That is not the day he will be free, but that day, he will be transferred to a new kind of prison which is much more frightening and nightmarish. Although his work is a place of confinement in itself, it is actually helping him and his family. Besides, no matter what goes on in his life, his office is where he finds himself distracted from all his life circumstances and thoughts that haunt him. Work makes him forget his sorrows, although it burns down his dreams and aspirations too. Work makes him tired and give him a good night's sleep. Atleast it used to.

Time is like free money, and most people don't know what to do with it.

After almost an hour of pushing time forward, Meera calls him. Gregor has a thousand thoughts flying about him before he accepts the call.

"Yes," Gregor says.

"I suppose today was the best day of your life."

Gregor simply listens without giving any response.

"The king visited the house of the common. Must be your best day."

Gregor stays silent, as if he is trying to communicate something with it.

"But, you don't seem happy about it," She says. "Dude, are you even on the call?"

Gregor does not open his mouth.

"Dude, I didn't expect that moron to fuck it up," she says. "What the fuck did he say? His brother did something idiotic in his childhood? Yeah everyone is like his stupid brother, right? And everyone is a suicidal child."

No response.

"Man, I don't know how many more times I will say sorry to you. Maybe I should say sorry to you once and for all. Like a single payment premium account," she says.

Silence.

"Hey, why am I giving a monologue? This is supposed to be a conversation. A dialogue."

"If you had told me that the boss is also coming, I would have prepared myself for whatever that came with it," he says. "It literally feels like getting unexpectedly hit by a truck. It hurts more than my accident, to be honest; to be told like that in front of my parents and sister, and you four, my colleagues. Imagine the humiliation my parents might have felt."

"It sucks, doesn't it?" she says. "A surprise gone wrong! It was a last minute thought, and how am I supposed to tell it to you on call with him by my side?"

Gregor goes silent again.

"Why the hell did I think that, that fucking pervert was coming along with us in good spirits? He simply came with us so that he can fuck everything up."

Silence.

"Man, this is now a monologue with interjections, not a dialogue. It still feels like I am talking to myself," she says. "Atleast curse me, just fucking open your mouth. I really can't handle silence."

Gregor still does not say anything. He has, within him, a lot of words filled with emotions, that he wishes he can articulate, but he is not able to open it up to her. He may not be angry with her, but at this point there is no one he can direct his anger to, and for most of his life, he has projected his anger mainly through silence, and that is clearly what he is doing at the moment. "Besides," Gregor says. "I wonder why he thinks that I intentionally created this accident, so that I can skip this stupid marketing event."

"His brother was a fucking psycho," Meera says, "and he thinks that everyone else in the world is like that. He is definitely a school boy stuck in an old man's body."

Gregor does not say anything.

"Anyways, do you want me to continue on call and say more dumb things or do you want me to go?"

"I have no problem with listening to your nonsense."

"And I have no problem with blabbering," she says. "Forgot to ask, how's your headache?"

"It's better now."

"You might be sleeping a lot, huh?"

"I slept so much that I woke up and I don't know what to do with my life."

"It happens," she says. "Happens with me too."

"I slept so much so that I don't know what's real and what's dream."

"Oh, that incident with the boss was definitely a nightmare, then."

Gregor chuckles. "I wish."

"Well, yeah. Some people are nightmare personified. Such people makes it difficult for us to lay a distinction between nightmare and reality."

"Some people do find pleasure in making the lives of others look nightmarish."

"Right," she says. "Man, but look, you really lead a lonely life. I thought your house would be flooded with visitors. It's like, you met with an accident, and nobody cares."

"I can't say that makes me unhappy."

"You love loneliness, don't you?"

"Sometimes it is the only thing that feels right," he says.

"Weird," she says. "Loneliness is good, as long as it doesn't fuck you up."

"But, I had a visitor today," he says.

"Who was it?"

"My cousin. I last saw her probably 22 years back."

"Sounds like a reunion."

"It was, and I am happy she visited."

"And that whale came to ruin that little bit of happiness you had," she says.

"Well, he succeeded in it, a bit," he says. "But, thinking about it, it still makes me happy. We always used to do one crazy thing or the other as kids."

"You sound happy, and I must admit I feel good about it."

CHAPTER THIRTY-THREE

For almost three years of his life, Gregor was in a loop where he used to wake up in the morning, get tired, and return to bed. Now, for the first time, there has been a break for rest, and Gregor is unsure how to handle it. Since he had slept for two long days, sleep does not come to him. He tries to sleep till almost three in the morning, to no result. He simply feels more awake than he ever was, the whole day. But unlike other nights devoid of sleep, he does not think like a maniac. Infact, his head feels empty and lightweight. He gets up from his bed, turns the light on, and walks towards the wash basin, like his habit. Sometimes, even Gregor's mind surprises him. Most of the time, his mind is that of a five year old who is afraid of everything, and at some rare moments like this, his mind is that of a sixty year old, who is not afraid of anything anymore, even death. Gregor makes up his mind so that whatever happens, tonight he will look at the face of the devil without any fear, like a stoic. His eyes are closed as he stands before the mirror. He opens them slowly, and what he sees in front of him brings tears to his eyes, which then starts rolling down. He wipes them off, but they still come without cease. What he sees in the mirror is his normal face which he has almost forgotten. He looks at his eyes, which are starting to get red. He has never seen how beautiful he is, but now, he feels happy about his facial features, his nose, his hair, his teeth, everything. His cheeks and jaw hold stubbles which have started tickling his face. He sees his smile for the first time in many days. His smile is something he rarely saw, even before he started having visions. He looks at his hands, his body and finally realises that he is finally reverted to his usual self. Happiness knows no bounds within him, and it feels as if an ocean which has always been within him, has its waves crashing as if in happiness. He smiles for one last time, at himself, turns the light off, and turns towards his bedroom. As he moves his foot back, it lands on something that feels like a cockroach, or a beetle, or some other insect that has accidentally tried to pass by. The crashing of the waves within him stops immediately, making the silent night more silent. The silence lets him hear the crunch of the tiny body crushing under his feat. Something nauseating starts rising from his underbelly and swiftly moves up within him. He does not take his foot off, or he can not, as if someone is stamping on top of his, preventing him from lifting it up. It crushes the insect more, maybe cutting its body into two. Gregor struggles but he finally succeeds in taking his foot off the insect. There arises a strange and sharp sound, probably from that insect, which may not be unusual in the ears of other people. But, for Gregor, it seems to deafen him. He covers his ears in horror, but it does nothing to prevent it from disturbing him and he falls sideways. He attempts to push his wrists furthermore into his ears to shut them well, so that no sound may creep in. He looks at where the insect is, and finds that it has grown in size, like the size of a human being on four limbs. It has a crushed body and it is writhing in pain. He lets out a scream, and someone in the house turns the lights on.

CHAPTER THIRTY-FOUR

The face he first sees upon waking up is that of his sister. She looks at him expectantly, as if waiting for him to open his eyes. Maybe she is the one who has woken him up, he does not know. He looks behind her at the wall clock, and finds that it is seven in the morning, the usual time when he wakes up on a normal workday. He slowly gets up from the bed. The pain in his ankle and head is down to minimal. He knows that he can stand up properly. Gregor does not look at his sister, and tries to avoid her eyes as much as possible, until it was impossible not to. When he casually turns towards his sister, she was staring at her, and her face looks sympathetic than angry.

"What happened to you last night?" She asks.

"I stepped on an insect and I fell down."

A smile blossoms on her face, and slowly she starts laughing. Gregor laughs too. "Aren't you a small baby!" She says. "And why did you scream?"

As she asks that question, Gregor gets flashes of what he had seen last night. He was on the floor, and the insect lying next to him had grown into the size of a man, and it was making that huge noise. Gregor shudders at that thought. His smile leaves his face in that instant. His sister sees this sudden change in his expression.

"What happened?" She asks.

"No, when I fell down, it hurt my leg, where it got injured." He points at his ankle. The bandage surrounding it is clean, and devoid of blood. It was clearly not the side that hit on the floor last night. He steals a glance at his sister, who he imagines, is thinking the same thing. "But, wasn't all that a dream?"

"I don't think mom is crying because she was in your dream last night."

"So, it was real?"

"I guess," she says. "I wasn't there. Mom explained it to me in the morning. I didn't even hear you scream."

"And mom is crying?"

"Yes."

"Why?"

"She seems happy for what has come unto her son."

"Where is father?"

"Reading the newspaper," she says. "Ah, I forgot, I actually came here to ask you whether you are going to work today. Mom sent me."

"I am definitely leaving. If I take leave for three days in a row, then my case is finished. Besides, I feel better now. The medicines have worked miracle,"

"Oh, I guess medicines did their work last night too. Maybe that is why you fell down."

"Don't bother. It is none of your business."

Her face turns into that of contempt. "As if I care."

"You better not. I have better people to care about me."

"It's good you fell down. I intentionally kept that insect there to trip you down, you little baby!"

"Did someone clear that insect from the hall?"

"I don't know. I don't care about your issues anymore. Your highness, why don't you get out of your chamber and go check by yourself?" She says and walks off. Gregor puts his head down, and then his sister suddenly appears at the door again. "Are you going to take your bandages off today, you invisible man? Or are you going to put on a show?"

"I thought you didn't care, and I don't want you to, either," Gregor says, turning back to look at her.

"Lemme thank my secret agent, again," she says.

"Your secret agent?"

"Yeah. The insect," she says.

"Ah, the insect, where is it?" He asks her, but she has already gone.

CHAPTER THIRTY-FIVE

After a few minutes of searching, Gregor finds the insect outside the house, by the back door. He watches as an army of ants takes it somewhere, probably to their kitchen. It looks like a wasp, and the body is damaged beyond recognition. Gregor does not want to disturb the ants, instead he simply looks at the scene as they carry it away with happiness. He gets inside the house. He does not have an eye contact either his father or mother, as he prepares for the bathroom.

CHAPTER THIRTY-SIX

He locks the bathroom door and suddenly stops acting. It is as if a mask has fallen from his face, immediately as he made an entrance. He sees it through his side glance first - his own reflection in the mirror. But he already knows without the mirror telling that the beast, which has gone on a trip for a night has returned in the morning. He brushes his teeth, without looking at the mirror, and as he finishes it, he strips naked, turns the shower on and lets himself get drenched. He has his eyes closed, his silent tears getting washed away. He has grown used to his insect body. He is neither surprised, nor desperate. After he finishes his shower, he wipes his body, and as he draped the towel round his waist, and open the door, he sees some movement behind the water closet. He is struck with terror. He starts trembling. He turns his head to his right, and finds that his worst fears have come true. He sees a life-size insect, hiding behind the water closet, afraid of him, trying its best not to be seen. Gregor's eyes widen, and he keeps himself from fainting. His whole body starts trembling as if the land beneath him is quaking. He cannot control his hands as he tries to open the door, but he finally succeeds in doing it. He gets out, slams the door shut and locks it. He finds that his heart is beating fast, and he is not stopped trembling yet. He tries to calm down, although he does not know how to get his composure back.

CHAPTER THIRTY-SEVEN

That night, before he tripped over the insect and made himself a laughing stock before his sister, Gregor was talking to Meera, his only friend these days.

"You know what," she said. "I was reading about coffee."

"Coffee?"

"Yeah. You like it?"

"Used to. I don't drink these days."

"Yes. Sometimes I forget that you're weird."

Gregor did not say anything.

"So, there's an interesting story behind the origin of coffee. It's probably just a myth, but who knows. But, listen to me. Back then, people had no idea what this coffee fruit was. So, there was this shepherd called Kaldi, who lived in Ethiopia, back in 400 AD or something. One day, while he was watching over his flock of goats, he found with surprise that a few of his goats were acting weird, you know. But they weren't weird like you. Instead, those goats seemed energetic and they were dancing like crazy. Kaldi was definitely surprised, he was like what the fuck? He went over and found that the goats were dancing under the influence of some kind of fruit. He might have been jealous of the dancing goats, I guess. So, he also plucked a fruit and consumed it. To his surprise, he also felt so energetic and started dancing."

"No way," Gregor interrupted. "Everyone is dancing in your story."

"I didn't write this story, man! Also, don't interrupt me. Let me finish it," she said and continued with it. "So, Kaldi. He understood that this is not some ordinary fruit. So he plucked a few and took it to a monk who lived nearby."

"And, he also danced?"

"Not too soon. The monk had one good look at the fruit and said that the fruit was nothing but the work of the devil and he threw them into the fire. But the magic happened as the coffee fruits started burning. They produced this captivating fragrance that bewitched the monk. Then, yes, he also started dancing, and he realised that it was not some ordinary fruit. You know, once you get bewitched with something, you always accept it, even if you think it's the Devil. But, I'm glad the monk finally accepted it. These monks and such can even change the scriptures they believe in, when it fails to work for them. The poor and confused always follow them, without knowing that these monks are also mortals, with limited time in this world. They make decisions, ensuring that the ground they stand on is safe and comfortable. I rather think that everyone should be allowed to make decisions for themselves. We boast freedom and are still captives of religion. But yes. in this story, the monk totally made the right decision. Otherwise, you know, I can't even imagine a life without coffee."

"But, I stopped caring," he said. "Be it religion or coffee, it doesn't matter to me anymore."

"You're a psycho," she said. "But, you know, the coffee machine in our office makes probably one of the best coffees I've ever drunk. I think, we must thank our boss for that."

"He installed it because we won't go out and waste time, or you know, have some quality time together."

"Yeah I do remember the scenes before he installed the coffee machine," she said. "But, the victory is ours. We got the best coffee."

"I've never tried it."

"You should, tomorrow. I'll drink with you."

"Let's see."

"Or simply stop talking to me. If you can't even do such a silly thing."

"But I don't think the goats, the shepherd and the monk actually danced because of a coffee fruit. It does bother me. I don't see people dancing after a cup of coffee."

"I believe they actually did," she said. "And these fruits, like everything else, lost their power over the years, I guess, except human beings."

Gregor stayed silent. There was silence on her part too. He thought that this is the part where she would hang up.

"Imagine Manu dancing," she suddenly said and laughed much longer than what was necessary. Gregor could only cringe to it.

Although Gregor did not get proper sleep that night, in the state of continuous unconscious and conciousness, he dreamt of coffee beans flowing like a river, and he was trapped in between, and at three o'clock in the morning, he woke up, thirsty for coffee.

CHAPTER THIRTY-EIGHT

"Does it still hurt?" Meera asks and attempts to touch the wound on his head. She almost succeeds in it thanks to Gregor shoving her hand away.

"Didn't you sleep last night?" Gregor asks, watching Meera yawn, as she stands before him holding the coffee cup. Her eyes slowly close, as if she is about to fall.

"No. I couldn't sleep, to be honest. Maybe because it was a Sunday. Sundays make me so empty," she says. "And that is where this coffee comes in." She shows him her coffee cup and takes a sip from it.

"I, on the other hand, had a good night's sleep," Gregor lies, and avoids meeting her glance, as if she will find out that he is lying. But, she is not looking at him. She does not seem to care.

"Of course," she says. "What have you got to think about?"

"Yeah, there is nothing." He smiles at her and takes his first sip too.

"Did you like it?" She asks.

"Not upto the hype created by you," he says. "But, it's too early to say. I will tell you once I finish it.

Meera grimaces and looks away. "Come, let's sit here and drink."

They walk to the coffee table nearby, and sit on adjacent chairs.

"Or, maybe it is not about Sundays," she says. " I don't get enough sleep these days. I try my best for two-three hours, and then I get up and walk inside my room, or listen to some music. Last night, I cleaned my desk, and the day before yesterday, it was my table. I clean my room at least twice a week. It's all because of this sleeplessness. I'm very tired, you know?"

"Maybe you should drink less coffee," he says, taking a sip.

"Maybe you should stop talking. What the hell do you know about coffees?" She says.

"What is there to know about coffees?"

"Oh, God! Asking you to have coffee with me was the biggest mistake I made in the last two years." Meera buries her head between her hands. Her hair is disheveled, and it seems as if she can fall on the table asleep, at any moment. She stays like that, and silence prevails.

Gregor feels the presence of someone behind him, and he also hears the hum of the coffee machine. Gregor turns back to find that it is his boss, which is strange because he rarely comes to the cafeteria, and most of the time, it is his personal assistant who gets his things done. Gregor has noticed before that his boss used to behave differently and out of his nature when women are around. He remembered that incident a few months back, when three senior women employees in the office asked Gregor whether he could come with them to have some tea from a cafe outside. That day, Gregor couldn't disagree with it, because, although they were his colleagues, he had never talked to them before, and nobody in the office had ever asked him to join for tea. So, that day, Gregor went to the boss' chamber to ask for permission to go out. The boss, on knowing who all were joining him, told, "Wait. I am also coming with you." Gregor had never seen his boss going out with any employee for tea during office hours. But, that day, he surprised everyone. He readied himself, so that he could walk with them to the cafeteria. Every single employee stopped their work for a few seconds and looked at him with wonder and considered it as an act of humility on his part. As they got out of the office, the three women walked together in front, the boss walked with Gregor chatting about office work and the personal assistant followed them. After the treat, the boss paid the bills. As they reached the office building, the women went on to have a chat with Gregor. The boss interrupted the chat with a joke, looked at the group of women, said, "He is a little flirt, right?", and laughed.

Gregor touches Meera's arm, to alert her. She opens her eyes, and gathers her composure, as she sees the man standing in front of her.

The boss turns to look at Meera and smiles at her. Then he looks at Gregor and his smile fades. "Why are you here?" He walks forward and stands by the table.

"I just thought of taking a coffee break," Gregor says.

"Didn't you get enough rest when you were on leave for two days?"

Gregor looks at him, out of words.

"Don't you have work to do?"

Gregor is silent.

"You thought you could spend the company time enjoying yourself?"

Still no answer.

"I know what your real problem is. You are a dumbass who don't know how to do any works. You are a zero in literally everything. Still, you think you can do chit-chats under my nose. You know what, I really don't want you here! You are simply wasting my time, space, money and now, like many times before, my energy," he says this and stops as if waiting to hear a response from Gregor. But Gregor stays silent, looking at his superior in his eyes; angry but forced to act guilty of a crime. "I can see it in your eyes, you loser. If you are so sexually frustrated, go work somewhere else."

He says this, and the next thing he knows is the hot coffee splashed on his face.

Gregor gets up stunned, and looks at Meera, who has done the act. Gregor is dumbstruck, and he stands without knowing what to do. He wonders if he should comfort Meera or his boss. But, instead of tending either of them, Gregor withdraws, taking steps backwards, pushing himself towards the wall, and behind the coffee machine. He watches both of them; Meera standing like a maniac, with her hair out of place; the boss with his head casted down, insulted. Both do not move for a few seconds, and for a moment, Gregor feels as if the only sound that remains in this world is that of his breaths and heart beats.

The boss then turns to Gregor with a straight face, and says in a calm voice. "You, come to my office."

CHAPTER THIRTY-NINE

"Do you regret what you've done?" Gregor asks, his fingers barely touching her leg. Meera does not react in any way. She simply sits on the park bench with her right hand covering her face which is already casted down. Gregor takes his hand back and keeps them crossed before him. He looks at the greenery in front of him, the families, friends, and couples who are probably having a great time, and the social reformer whose statue is placed at the center of the park. The park is named after him.

Gregor leans back. He does not know why he asked the question he just did. Although the answer to the question is evident, he really wants to know what she thinks about what she has done. Also, he knows that she is someone who believes in her actions. But, things seem to contradict each other, and now Gregor really wants to know: does she regret what she has done?

Silence now has arms, and they start to strangle him. He looks forward, but he's also noticing any movement on her side. She seems to be as lifeless as the statue of the reformer. Then she starts shaking. The movement is so slow but Gregor notices it. He looks at her and realises that she is weeping. He feels embarrassed for a moment that people around him have also started looking at them. A person crying is always a curious picture. What is it that makes them cry? We will start making assumptions. We will smile at it, and satisfy ourselves thinking that it happened to them, but not us; it makes them cry but we are not even remotely affected it. We prefer to know what makes them sad than what makes them happy. We are forever in our pursuit of sadness.

"Meera?" He tries to calm her down. "Why are you crying? Don't be afraid. I know that you are capable of doing something bigger and better. Moreover, like you said, it's not a big thing to work for Manu."

Meera raises her head from her hand and looks at him. Her eyes are bloodshot, and her hair is dishevelled like before. She now looks like something similar to a breathing ghost. "I am not afraid of what is going to happen to me," she says. "I am afraid of what is going to happen to you. You don't even have the courage to die!" Each of the words of her are but stones thrown to his heart. For a moment, Gregor feels as if it is really a ghost, not Meera, that talks to him.

After the happenings at the cafeteria, Gregor was called into the boss' chamber. Although it was Meera who had thrown coffee on his face, it was Gregor who got fired, and the boss took no action against Meera. "You are the reason behind every fucking thing that goes wrong in this office. You are but a bad omen, a negativity. Even Meera, who threw the coffee on me, does not deserve any retributions, because she, unlike you, does her job pretty well, and if she threw any coffee on my face she did it under your fucking influence. I am sure that the office is only going to fare better if you leave. You are fired! Now, get the fuck off from my room!"

Gregor did not leave the office right then. He instead waited in the reception, apparently waiting for his boss to call him to his cabin and tell him that he had reconsidered his decision. But, he waited in vain. After that, Gregor did try to meet the boss a few times, but he couldn't even get the glimpse of the big man.

Meera, considering the embarrassment of working in the office under a man who she had assaulted, gave in her papers, although the boss had tried his best to show her that he has forgiven her, by often smiling at her, and even going towards her seat and explaining himself. "I am not angry with you. That guy is not required in the office, at all. He has always failed to prove his mettle and on the last day he didn't even attend our marketing event. Firing him was already in the cards and that's why I had talked to him the way I did in the cafeteria. He deserves it. That's what he is, and that's where he stands." She swiftly moved her hand and clutched her water bottle which had no cap. The boss, took a sudden step back, understanding what she meant. He stared at her, although she was not looking at him, and he walked back to his cabin in anger. After that, she got up, walked to the HR room and told the other big man in the office that, "I quit this fucking office." She then walked out of the HR room, packed her things and met Gregor at the reception. She stood by the office door and looked at him. "There is no use waiting here. Come." Gregor understood the truth in her words, and walked towards her. Together they walked out of the office building and found their way towards this park nearby.

"I don't regret what I have done. I will never do that, I promise," she says. "It just makes me horribly sad thinking that I might have just ruined your life."

Gregor is out of words. He bites the nail folds of his right hand, and with his other hand, he tries to pluck them off.

"I don't know." Gregor does not cry, although he wants to. "Afterall, it is just a job. We move out of one job, enter another, it is as simple as that. There is nothing to cry about it."

Meera wants to speak, but her voice does not come out. Her eyes look pink, and her mascara has spread underneath her eyes. Her hair is still dishevelled, and Gregor sees a broken woman in front of him. She continues to stare at him.

"You need to stop thinking about me. I am sure I will manage, no matter what," he says. "You should go wash your face and do your hair."

"I am leaving," she says and gets up, ready to leave.

"Sure," Gregor says, but instead of waiting for his reply, she walks towards the park gate. "Take care," Gregor whispers to himself. Then he looks at the social reformer, who is standing tall; the only person who is looking back at him, at the moment. There is nothing to see here. Gregor shrugs.

CHAPTER FORTY

Yesterday was not the first time when Gregor saw that huge insect in his house. It was many years ago; one night when he was just about to sleep. Half an hour after he laid down, closing his eyes, he felt a gentle touch on his back. It was more like the touch of a human. When he looked back, he saw this huge insect trying to climb on him. Half of its legs were on the floor, and the other half on his back. The bug seemed bigger and stronger than him. Gregor immediately shook that insect off him, and in a shock, he moved backwards, hitting himself in the wall. He saw the insect, terrified like him, moving back, and he saw the insect crawling underneath his bed. Gregor started a cry, calling out for his mother and father, who came to the room within a minute. They opened the room, turned on the light and saw Gregor sitting on the bed, still crying out loud, his face wet with tears.

"What happened, boy?" His mother immediately rushed to him, and held him inside her hands, closing him into her chest.

"I saw a ghost," he said, looking at his mother. "I swear on you, I saw it. It is under the bed."

His mother turned towards her husband and passed him a harsh stare that could pierce through him.

His father, defeated, could only look at his wife, without knowing what he must say, deliberating the reason for her piercing stare. He got on his knees, looked under the bed and said, "There's nothing here. He must've had some bad dreams."

"I saw it. I swear. It looked so devilish. I saw its face. It looked like a huge insect," Gregor kept on muttering.

His mother was still staring at her husband. Her eyes were red, and her face, fresh with tears. "How many times did I tell you not to choose this haunted house, where a madman once lived a lonely life and killed himself? You chose this just because no one had even dared to come and check out this damned house. Now see, the madman's ghost is here now, disturbing our son. Does that make you happy? I suppose it does."

His father got up from the floor. "Talk with some sense, Priya. Who the hell believes in ghosts these days? It was nothing but a bad dream."

"Me. I believe in ghosts, and tonight my son saw it in his room. How the hell can you not believe him when he is swearing on me with tears?" His mother was raging at him, clutching Gregor even closer.

His father looked at his son and wife. He stood with his hands on his hips, contemplating. Out of the many little memories Gregor has from the past, the image of his father standing on the backdrop of the purple walls, is something that still continues to stay with Gregor.

"You are-" His mother started again.

"Alright, fine. Please, Priya," his father said, gesturing to his wife to stop talking. "No more arguments on this. We will be vacating this week. It's my promise."

Although they shifted to a different house that week, as promised by his father, it didn't even have a least impact on his mother's passion for ghosts. She continued to believe every other ghost story that she heard, and shared it to Gregor like a fervent storyteller. His father never came to know about this—he was not even aware of his wife's situation, for that matter—so he could never try and dissuade Gregor from his belief in ghosts. The sight of a ghost only strengthened his conviction that they do exist. After that, although he was blessed with a peaceful sleep every night, even small sounds in and around his house, made him wake up with a start. At first, he used to cry out for his mother, then slowly as he grew up, he started managing things on his own, like turning the lights on, and looking for a presence of someone or something. He used to check every corner in his room, taking atleast twenty minutes, before returning to sleep.

CHAPTER FORTY-ONE

Gregor is reluctant to leave the park, since he does not know what he shall do afterwards. He takes out his phone, plugs in his earphones, and tries to amuse himself with things which are not real. But, they fail to make an impression on him. He calls his mother, thinking that he should deliver the news first before going face to face with her. His mother takes the call right before the last ring. As usual, it takes her at least ten seconds to say "hello" since she may have attended the call, while she was doing something else.

Although his mother said a "hello", he does not know what to say in response or how to start talking to her. He takes more time than her for a response.

"Should I get anything for home?" Gregor instead asks, finally, after almost five seconds of silence.

"You sound different. I know you didn't call to ask me that," she says. "Don't you remember that you have to go out with your sister this evening? She said she got some things to buy."

"Yeah. I almost forgot about that supermarket thing."

"You always forget such things."

"But mom, I'm not..." he says and stops short.

"I'm not...?

"Nothing. Forget it."

"Alright," she says. "You left early today?"

"I will be leaving in an hour. Normal time." The word normal continues to stay with him even after he has uttered it.

"Tell me, son. What happened? Something is amiss in your voice."

"Nothing happened."

"But you never—"

"I am at work. I will call you back." Gregor raises his voice a bit, and a family, a man, woman and a little girl, who are passing by, turn to look at him, surprised. The little girl smiles at him, as if making fun of the fact that he just lied that he was at work. He cuts the call and looks at them apologetically.

CHAPTER FORTY-TWO

Gregor waits in the park for an hour more, passing time, looking at his phone, and the myriad of people who come and go in the park. Although it is crowded, no one comes and sits next to him. He realises that even parks are not for lonely people for they can only leave after having their mind tortured, watching people relish their moments of togetherness. He wonders if he had acted in a better way then Meera would have stayed. But he realises that he does not know what the better way is. His phone's battery almost runs out thirty minutes before six. So, he locks it and puts it back into his pocket. He holds on to the thought to run away from this and everything else, till the watch says six o' clock. He gets up and walks towards the railway station. He feels as if there is no energy left in him; as if he will fall down midway.

On the way, he passes by the lonely river where people only come to die. He has passed by it a million times, but had never really stopped to watch it flow. Although the river only witnesses the death of barely one person every year, it is still considered as a river of the suicides, probably due to some major incident in the past, who cares? Because of which, no one really visited the river, making it flow alone, carrying the ghosts. Probably, what terrified the people is not the ghosts of the dead, but the ghosts of their thoughts. He passes the hedges of the river, reaches the bank and stands there watching the river flow, peacefully. He finds it with surprise that no one is there to dissuade him from a probable suicide attempt. He wonders how easy it is to die there. Watching the trees on the other side of the river, the birds flying peacefully, the sea weeds, his eyes finally land on his own reflection in the river

— The big ugly insect that makes people cringe with disgust.

CHAPTER FORTY-THREE

"Buy anything you want," Gregor says. "And you pay the bill too."

His sister lands a punch on his belly and he groans, covering his belly with both his hands to prevent further attack. "Do I have to suffer these tortures and still have to pay for everything you buy?"

"Yes. That you should."

"You know what, I made a mistake bringing you here today."

"You're wrong, little boy." She stops walking with her trolley and smiles at him. "I brought you here. Not the other way round." She then continues her walk through the aisle.

His nose catches some strong smell and Gregor tries to remember where that familiar smell comes from.

"Do you smell something weird?" Gregor asks her as they walk through the aisle of utensils and office stationery.

She stops and sniffs. Her face changes. "You haven't had a bath in seven days, did you?"

"Damn you, you little devil," he says, hitting her on the side of her upper arm.

She hits him back. "And you are the biggest psychopath."

"You do your shopping," Gregor says. "I'm going to have a little detour."

He comes out of that aisle and takes his phone out. He calls Meera, and in the meantime, he sniffs the smell more into his nostrils trying to identify what it is. Still, no idea. He walks in front of different aisles, slowly, listening to the never-ending rings, which then ends. Gregor stops and opens WhatsApp and types a message to Meera. "Hey. Did you reach home? How are you doing now?" The message is sent and it shows that she has also received it. Gregor realises that he has reached the aisle of foods. So he enters in, and looks at the rate of different snacks and biscuits, and immediately puts them back. Still, he browses through them. He knows that his sister will be buying something, so he does not get anything for himself.

Gregor checks his phone again, at the message he has sent. There are blue ticks under his message, but still, there is no reply yet. He waits for some more time for a reply and sends another text. "Hey? Are you alright?" She views the message instantly. Gregor locks the phone, keeps it in his hands, and continues browsing. His eyes are on the phone, waiting for it to blink, which it does, in a few minutes. Gregor immediately opens her message, and a strange current passes through him. She has sent three messages. "Let's not talk again", "I'm sorry", "Bye." Gregor frowns at the message, confused. Now, he has seen the message and he does not know how to respond to it. He looks at the phone screen until the brightness goes dim. He has a packet of snacks in his other hand, and for a moment, he feels nauseous seeing it.

He keeps it back and that familiar smell returns to him. This time, the odour is so severe that it overwhelms his olfactory sense and almost pulls him down. He loses control, moves back, and almost hits the aisle below, but he catches himself before he can create much damage. The odour... Is it the odour of green apples? In a super market, the smell of green apples is pretty normal, especially when he is standing nearby the fruit stall. That is when the buzz came. Like the sound of a million bees, a much stranger and stronger version of the sound he had heard the last night as he laid next to the giant insect.

Gregor struggles to cover his nose and ears with both his arms, as he walks towards where the sound was coming from, which was behind the snacks section. He reaches the next aisle and peeps at what was going on. What he sees there terrifies him. He saw huge insects on the rows where products are supposed to be. They are moving their body, as if they are impatient with something. Watching them run through the rows, freezes him for a few seconds. He covers his mouth in terror and tries to move back, hitting the row behind him.

"What happened?" The voice of his sister snaps him off from the hallucination. He still looks terrified as he watches his sister walk towards him. Her face has a concerned expression, which further intensifies as he reaches nearby him. "Do you see something there? You look like you saw an actual ghost." She says, as she reaches near him.

He looks at the rows, where he had seen the insects earlier. He understands that he was hallucinating. His sister looks in the direction of his gaze, at the rows, and her face now looks even more worried.

"What in the world is going on?" She asks. "Now you are terrified of some silly teddy bears?"

O

CHAPTER FORTY-FOUR

There was a time, sometime in his school days, when Gregor went missing. As said earlier, Gregor was only an average student in school, but there was one thing that he was really good at: Quizzes. He was so passionate about questions and their answers. As a child, he was so curious about things, that he used to ask questions, to which he got no correct answers in return. So he started reading books, and he saved money to buy quiz books, specifically. He did not care about his textbooks, but he was interested in everything else.

One day, the class teacher revealed to the whole class about a quiz tournament that was happening in a far away place. "A quiz team consists of two students. You can choose your partner by yourself. Only one team from each school can attend this tournament. So, on Friday, there will be a selection process for all the teams that are participating from this school. Those interested should report to me by this afternoon. Heard?" She said to the whole class, and turned to look at Gregor specifically, with a smile. He smiled back at her.

After she said, all eyes were on Gregor, and Gregor had his eyes on the rest of the class. He had to choose one of them, but he had no friends. He was also inhibited to go towards them and ask them if they could be his partner. But soon to his relief, a guy stepped up.

"You just have to come with me," Gregor said, with the stammer he had back then, which came to him at first as a result of his lack of self confidence. "I can't promise that we will be the team that gets selected, but I'm so passionate about this. I really want to participate. You just have to be with me, as a partner."

"I know," the boy said, his thin face radiating the most beautiful smile. "I'm there with you."

That Friday, there was an intense competition that started from the morning, which ended a little long after the school hours. Gregor felt as if his head was on fire. He skipped his lunch due to the stress, although his team was winning. In the final, there were only two teams, including Gregor's. That day, his team finally defeated the other team, and became worthy of travelling to the Quiz championship. When the selection was over, the school was desolate. Only both the teams, and two teachers who had the responsibility of conducting the tournament remained. Leaving them behind, Gregor and his friend rushed to the washroom. They reached the washroom, and checked themselves in the big mirror placed by the door.

"Now that I helped you, I expect a favour from you too." His friend said, as he was combing his hair.

"You helped me?" Gregor said.

The boy shot a look. "Didn't I? Nobody in the class was ready to join you. Only I did. Consider that as my generousity."

"Okay," Gregor nodded, looking at the mirror and doing his hair with his fingers. "But, what is it that you want?"

"I want you to leave our team."

"Leave our team?" Gregor said, stealing a glance at him through the mirror. The boy was looking at him back. "What are you saying?"

"Be a good friend and return my favour, so that I can ask those teachers whether I can add Ishita in, instead of you."

"What do you mean Ishita?"

"We've never gone out anywhere. Our parents won't allow it. But if there's a quiz tournament, then they have no option but to agree. Moreover, it's in a faraway place. We can have some quality time together, man. They say, a friend in need is a friend indeed. I showed up when you were in need. Now, you should do the same."

"You are asking for the impossible," Gregor said. "It's something that I love doing. I can't just give it up for this."

"You should. Otherwise, I will leave."

Gregor gave out a small laugh. "As if I care. You can leave, I'll ask the teachers to find a replacement for you."

The boy seemed fuming. He was staring at Gregor, who was smiling as if it was a joke.

"You then do it on your own. You fucking ungrateful pig." The boy said, storming out of the washroom.

The smile vanished from Gregor's face. Sorrow overwhelmed him suddenly. For a moment, he wondered if he was being ungrateful, and then he came to the conclusion that he sure was. He wanted to follow him and reach a settlement. But, the tension inside his bladder was much stronger than what was in his mind. He made an attempt to go behind him, then decided to use the toilet instead. He got inside the toilet and locked the door. He unzipped his pants and started relieving himself. He saw a cockroach behind the bucket, but he tried to remain cool, so as not to disturb it. That's when he heard a sound, as if the door was being latched from the outside. Terror shot up through his chest.

"You rot in there, stubborn asshole!" The boy shouted from the outside.

Gregor zipped his pants. In the sudden panic that ensued, he banged on the door violently. "Don't! Don't do this. This is not sensible. Open the door please! PLEASE!"

"Stay the night in there and tomorrow come back to me with a changed mind... Got it?"

Gregor heard the door of the washroom being closed and getting latched, like a final nail hammered on his coffin. "Don't do this! Open the door please! Please!" Gregor repeated this chant in vain. Gregor is normally soft-spoken, and there was a limit to how loud he could cry, so his sound did not go past the bathroom door, and even if it did, there was no one in the school to hear him. His friend might have probably been the last person to exit the school, and he might have already done so.

Gregor tried to knock and push the wooden door open with all his might, but it was all in vain. The panic in him had started panicking the cockroach too, which then began roaming around. Tears started streaming down his cheeks realising that there was nothing else he could do. He sat on the water closet and looked at the only insect in the toilet other than him, which had by then found a hiding spot in a corner behind the bucket comfortably, while Gregor found himself trembling in fear. His eyes were always on the insect, judging its movements. He got up without making any noise, and inched towards it. He slowly raised the empty bucket and moved it, so as not to disturb his resting friend. He came near the cockroach and raised his leg, in order to land his black, polished boot on it, but he missed it. The cockroach, on the other hand, spread its wings and flew up towards his face. He jerked back, slipped on the wet floor and fell back, hitting his head on the water closet.

The next thing he knew was the smell of a hospital and the murmur of people around him.

"Do you know who locked the door from outside?" His father asked him.

Gregor looked at the tired face of his father, with his half-open hazy eyes. He shook his head. "I've no idea."

"Do you know how worried we were?" His mother said.

"If it was a little longer, then you could have died."

"I feel better now," he said. "Mom, don't cry."

"Do you... do you have any doubt on who it could be?"

Gregor shakes his head again.

"You should at least give us two or three names. This isn't a small matter."

Within him, he still believed that it was all his fault. Friends are supposed to return favours, and he had been too stubborn. It was clearly his fault. Maybe, he should change his mind now, at least for his own sake.

Gregor did not go to the tournament, allowing his friend to go with his girlfriend. They failed in the tournament, of course, but after that boy became good friends with him, like nothing ever happened between them and they continued this friendship till they seperated ways, after many years.

Three months passed after the sighting of the giant bug in his house, the day Gregor got fired from the office and the day Meera last talked to him. Such a fateful day, the day when everything changed. Although, Gregor had tried to contact her through different ways, nothing was rendered fruitful. She was still away in silence.

He wakes up with music in his ears, which had been his ritual for over a month. He decides to remain on the bed, with the music filling his ears. He closes his eyes and relaxes himself, like every other day, for he does not have anywhere to rush to. He waits for the music to finish, so that he can finally get up. The music lasted for a few more minutes until it finally came to a halt.

Despite the coldness of the day, he feels hot, and pulls at his clothes, which weren't there. He shall get dressed, to make the appearance. He gets up, and as usual looks under his bed. He says good morning to his friend there. He stands before his wardrobe and looks at the mirror. He only looks at his disfigured face and not at his disfigured, yet healthy-looking body. He takes a shirt and a pant from the wardrobe and puts them on. He starts to perspire in the sudden heat that overwhelms him. He does his invisible hair in front of the mirror and smiles, which does not get reflected in the mirror. The smile vanishes from his face too.

He looks at the clock, and finds that it is nine in the morning. He makes a mental note to wake up a bit earlier. Although he has got nothing to do that early, he realises that wake up late is doing him no good, either.

As he walks towards the bedroom door, the giant bug that sleeps under the bed, runs towards his side. Gregor notices it. He smiles.

He unlocks the door, and knocks on it, so that someone will unlock it from the other side. "Mom, I woke up. Can you open the door now?" He calls out. He then, turns to look at the giant bug and whispers and motions with his hand. "Wait."

The door is unlocked from the other side. Gregor knows that he can only open the door a few seconds after it is fully unlocked. So he waits for five to ten seconds before opening the door. There is no one in the dining room. His father is nowhere to be seen. He sees his mother in the kitchen, as usual, with the electric bat in her hand, staring at him, as if he is a murderer. He passes a smile at her. Fear is painted on her face.

"Where is sister?" He asks. He has a stammer, and it takes him some time to finish his sentence.

"Why are you asking about her?" She retaliates.

He still smiles at her. He then turns away and walks towards the bathroom, the giant insect following him in.

CHAPTER FORTY-SIX

He comes out of the bathroom to find that his breakfast is not served on the dining table, which is unusual. On other days, his mother would have kept something edible for him on the table.

Gregor walks up to the kitchen, and stands outside, preparing to ask her. He knows that she will not let him in. His mother suddenly appears at the door and she pulls herself back, as if Gregor has given her a jumpscare.

"Muh-mother you-you should stop treating me like thi-this."

She brings a finger to her lips. "You want food right? I've kept it in your room. Your father has asked me not to allow you into the dining room."

"One apple?" He asks, looking at the giant bug standing by his side.

"Yes."

"I've told you I need two," he says, annoyed, still looking at his friend.

"Where's the money?" she asks

Gregor looks at her confused.

"Where do you think we get the money for an apple? Do you have any idea how hard we work for it? You only sit in your room and ask for another apple. Where's the money for that? Do you have it?"

"It's not like I'm not searching for jobs."

"Who do you think will give you a job, with that unstable mind of yours? I think it's a service to the world in itself if you just stay inside your room and choose not to work."

Gregor puts his head down. "If I'm a retard then take me to some hospital."

She again asks him to be silent with her finger on lips. She raises the electric bat in her other hand and motions towards his bedroom. "Your apple is kept there. Go have it."

"At least give me a knife to cut it into two," he says.

"You think I want to get killed?"

Gregor looks at her with his eyes watering up. Her eyes are red with rage.

She goes back into the kitchen and returns with a knife and gives it to him. He gets it from her. He walks to his bedroom and returns with the stale-looking apple that was kept on the bed. The giant insect was following him to and fro. He keeps the apple on the dining table and cuts it into two. He sees the brown patches of rot on it. He then gives the knife back. As he returns it, he finds her hand trembling. She looks afraid too. She is not looking at him. He smiles at what life has brought him to.

"I'll go back to my room."

"Go! Go!" she says, motioning her hands, shooing him away.

Gregor gets to his room and locks the door. He then hears the door getting locked from the other side. He sits on his bed, and the insect pushes itself underneath the bed. He looks at the pieces of the stale apple in both of his hands. He keeps one piece of it under the bed. As he eats the apple, he looks around his dirty room, which has not been cleaned in two months. After finishing the apple, he gets up from the bed and kneels down. He sees the insect sitting behind a heap of rotten apples. The apple he had just placed, remains there, untouched. He picks it up and tries to feed the insect. "Eat.. Eat.." But, it does not listen to him. So, he keeps the apple back and gets up, and sits on the bed again. He takes his mobile from the bed, and stares at the screen which is almost fully broken. If it were three months before, he would have rushed to the mobile shop to fix it; even a small scratch used to irritate him.

He surfs through different job apps and applies for those jobs that he finds suitable. Then he keeps the mobile to his side, and lays back, looking at the fan which has stopped working. His phone lights up for a call notification. But he does not see it, because it is on silent mode. Without having much to do with his day or his life, he closes his eyes. After probably an hour, he wakes up again. He feels uncomfortable in heat and inaction. He pulls at his hairs, and makes noises. He then removes his shirt and pants and spreads himself on the bed, trying to ward the never-ending heat off.

It is by night that he checks his phone again. He finds that Meera has tried to contact him twice, but he does not call her back.

Next morning, he wakes up again with the music in his ears. He stays on the bed till the music gets over, gets up, puts on his dresses, waits for his mother to open the door, get freshened, have a piece of apple with the other piece on the floor, surfs through those job apps and checks whether he has gotten any mails or messages. No one wants him. But then, the call notification pops up. It is Meera again. He wonders what it is that she wants from him. Is he even useful in some manner? Is she calling him to ask for money? Gregor has a thousand thoughts. By this time which he spent contemplating, the call gets disconnected, and Gregor heaves a sigh of relief.

Towards evening, Gregor hears the calling bell ring. He sharpens his ears. He can hear a conversation happening there, but he is not able to understand what they are talking about. But, he identifies her voice. Meera. He looks at the door to his bedroom, waiting for someone to come there and open the door. But no one arrives. After sometime the voices subside, and it becomes night. Gregor is still in the same position, watching the door. In the night, he gets the whiff of something spicy from the outside. As the aroma slowly fills the room, and his body, he feels intense hunger, making his stomach a furnace. He goes to sleep after emptying the water bottle and he feels as if his body is on fire, inside out.

Sometime into the midnight, maybe by two am, he hears faint knocks on the door, and the door gets unlocked. Gregor gets up immediately and puts on his clothes. He unlocks the door on his side, and opens it, to see his sister on the other side. He looks into her eyes, and she is looking back at him.

"Are you feeling hungry?"

Gregor nods, his eyes wet. He looks as if he'll cry with another word of hers.

"Here," she says, extending a plastic lunch box towards him. Gregor gets it from her, and looks at his sister for one last time, since he is seeing her after a long time.

"I hear your songs every morning," Gregor says. "I hope your students understand what you teach."

She does not say anything to that insult. She just smiles at him.

"And how is father?" Gregor asks.

"He seems tired," she says. "With all the work."

Gregor nods. "I don't know when it'll all get normal."

"I heard father say that we need to accept that things won't go back to normal. But, how judgemental are they? I'm sure things will be fine soon."

"It's not going to happen in this room. I need to get out. Get some help."

"I think they don't want you to be in a mental hospital. One part of father wants you to get you somewhere. But, mother is so against it, and he thinks that she is right. It's better for their reputation if you just stay in this room. They have told our relatives that you are working, somewhere far away."

"I know," Gregor says. "I was just telling you that things won't get better this way."

Her face is blank. She stands still, without knowing how to respond.

"What's more hurtful is how they have suddenly become so ungrateful."

"For that matter, they've never been grateful to you. They just enjoyed what you did. It is what it is. We can't change the way they think."

Gregor nods. "I'm losing my mind here."

"I don't know how I can help you."

"I suppose you have better things to think about. I'm not asking for help," he says. "Ok then, you go to sleep before father wakes up.

He gets up every now and then."

She nods.

Gregor closes the door, and locks it. He hears the door getting locked from the outside. He keeps a share for the insect underneath the bed, then sits on the chair and starts eating like a madman.

CHAPTER FORTY-SEVEN

That day, after he got fired, Gregor struggled for days to break that news to his family. To make them believe a false narrative, he used to wake up like usual, get dressed, eat breakfast, and got out of the house, as if it was just a regular day, and nobody doubted him. He used to roam in shopping malls, empty movie theatres, through streets where no one would spot him, and whenever he did not know what to do, he used to stand by the lake of the suicides, and simply watch the river flow. Gregor was so used to the comfort of a job, that once he was out of it, he did not know what to do. But, never once, even when he was standing by the lake, did he think about ending his life. It was not even a possibility for him. There were days when he used to go in front of his office building, just to have a look at it and imagine the life he missed. He could not believe that it was all for a girl, who ended up being nothing in his life. He would come back home and cried his heart out. He tried to protect the news for almost a month, until one night when he returned home soaking wet. That night, it was raining heavily, and Gregor was fed up being outside, doing things that helped him in no manner.

"I got fired," he told his mother, as if shooting her in the point blank.

"What for?"

"He had some disagreements with me, and today he finally asked me if I could leave. I knew that it was going to happen sometime soon. You know about his issues with me. Moreover, he is egoistic and selfish."

Gregor could not explain more. It was like, if he had opened his mouth for another time, then he would have cried. He instead held his composure, although something was breaking from within him.

Days of gloom started from there. Gregor did not have to act anymore. He had the privilege to wake up late, and simply answer to any questions held at him with a simple, "I am searching for a job." His parents, understanding the situation, started going for jobs with little income, hoping that Gregor will start working soon. His sister convinced her parents to start giving music lessons for children in and around the town. It was a long time dream of hers and since money was a necessity, her parents could only agree. Since then, Gregor wakes up to this melodious music, the only good thing in his life these days.

Those days , the only thing that remained constant in his life, was the rate at which insects grew inside his brain. After the sighting of the giant bug in the bathroom, he started noticing that it was following everywhere he went, and when he came to his bedroom, the bug just rested underneath his bed. Although, he was afraid of that creature at first, he slowly realised that it was as scared as him. So, he started being gentle with it.

"You and I," once he told the insect. "We are just the same."

It was during the same time that Gregor started feeling humid—despite what the weather was—triggering his allergy to heat. He did not share it with anyone, even with his mother, for it seemed like she was no more interested in his affairs. His entire body started itching, and when he tried to scratch on them, he felt hives - on his back, hands and legs. He started wearing long sleeved shirts, and pants, hiding his body from others. On days when it rained, he used to sit by the window, watching the downpour, imagining himself lying naked on the road, getting soaked, getting at least a temporary relief from the heat which was slowly burning him. Whenever he went to take a bath, he used to curl himself up underneath the shower, feeling the heat go off him, until someone knocked on the door, to vacate.

One day, while no one was at home, he stripped himself, ran to the bathroom, and turned the shower on. He did not even care to turn the lights on or lock the door. He stayed there for hours and hours, until the water ran out. The downpour from the shower was so comfortable that he found himself sleeping on the wet bathroom floor. Some time into the evening, his sister returned from college. She knocked on the main door for sometime, to no response. She then used the spare key she had and opened the door. She searched for him all over the house, only to find him nowhere. She found that the bathroom door was open and there was no light either. So she turned the light on and looked in. She let out a scream, seeing her brother sleeping naked on the bathroom floor. His body was disfigured with bruises and bumps. That scene almost traumatised her. It was that scream that woke him up. When their mother returned, she found her daughter shivering in terror. Gregor had closed himself inside his room, ashamed of what he had done. His mother locked the door from outside that day, and since then, Gregor is nothing but a prisoner in his own room. Since then, his mother stopped going to work, so that the girl would not be alone in the house with her mad brother.

CHAPTER FORTY-EIGHT

Gregor wakes up with music in his ears and continues to stay on the bed till the music is over. He gets up, walks to his cupboard and wears a good dress. He then unlocks the door and knocks on it. He waits for someone to open it from the other end. The door is fully unlocked. He waits for a few seconds, and opens the door. He looks at his mother, who was looking back at him from the kitchen, with the mosquito bat in her hands.

"I have a job interview today," Gregor tells her.

"Who in the world is so crazy enough to give you a job?"

"Let me leave."

"Go wherever you want, and don't come back," she says.

CHAPTER FORTY-NINE

No one in the world is crazy enough to give him a job. An interview is just an excuse for him to get out of his house imprisonment. He has nowhere to go. He gets out, walks the road he is used to, gets into a train, and walks the usual road to his workplace and stands outside, remembering his not-so-good yet not-so-manic life. He then walks back, passes by the park of the social reformer, looks at the crowd and remembers how he did not fit in. He then heads towards the river, the only place that gave him comfort.

He stands by the rails, looking down at the river, only to see a girl, dressed in a white frock standing in his usual spot. We don't know the name of the girl. So, let's just call her O. But, whatever her name is, Gregor feels something inside him say that she is there to meet her end. He runs down towards the river and stands behind her. He is unsure of what to do or say. He instead stands there simply, watching the river with her. She has a white rose in her hand, and she is plucking the petals off and throwing it in the river. She notices his presence, and she acknowledges it by turning to his side, looking at him briefly.

"I'm here to jump," she says. "Don't try to save me."

"I don't know how to swim either," he says.

"Are you here to jump too?"

He looks at her face clearly. She is pale, with eyes sunk in a dark pit. Her hair is loose and she is picking at it with her dirty nails. She looks like someone who once looked beautiful.

"Maybe," Gregor says. "I'll jump if you give me company."

"I should not care," she says. "But, if you have got at least a reason to live, don't give up."

"What makes you so hopeless, then?" Gregor asks.

"I killed my lover," she says. "I literally killed him. Now, the police are behind me."

Gregor turns to look at the river, and he wonders why it did not surprise him.

"Sometimes, killing someone is necessary too, isn't it?" Gregor finds himself saying.

She shoots a look at him. "I didn't kill him because it was a necessity. It's because of my vengeance."

"Vengeance." Gregor sighs.

"Yes."

"And what did he do to deserve your vengeance?"

"He killed my father," she says. "My father is the only person I have, besides my brother, and my now ex-lover. When he killed my father, I lost the two most important people in my life. It pushed me into madness, and finally this. Maybe in another version of my story, written by someone else, I'd have killed myself first."

"How did he kill your father, and why?"

"It's a long story," she says. "But he killed my father out of his vengeance too. I now understand how that emotion works within us. But only he has vengeance?" She looks at Gregor, as if he is the lover in question.

"Definitely not. I would say, what you did is right."

"There's no right in this story," she says, turning away from him. "It's all badly twisted."

Both stay silent for some time. He looks at the white petals falling into the river and getting carried away.

"There's a river like this that flows in my place. That's where we used to spend our private moments. Today I met him there for the last time. He also didn't know how to swim."

"The police are behind you?"

"They will be here any moment," O says. "Before that I should jump."

"Or you can place your trust in the law and believe that you will be acquitted of your crime, because you clearly look like a troubled mind."

"Get acquitted and return to this world which feels more horrific than prison? No, I don't wish to live," she says. She turns back and extends the rose towards him. He gets it from her. "Thanks for the conversation." Before allowing herself to finish her last word, she jumps into the river.

Gregor does not move or even stop her. He instead takes the mobile out of his pocket, and calls the police.

CHAPTER FIFTY

What Gregor did not notice at first is the fact that the giant bug, the permanent resident underneath his bed, has also left the house with him, and it is following him everywhere he goes. Gregor did not see it leave with him, or even walk with him in the streets. But, he did see the insect now and then, hiding here and there and while Gregor was with O, he thought he saw the insect hiding behind a bush. The insect is clearly afraid of everyone—everyone except Gregor.

After the police came, rescued O, and returned with her, Gregor leaves the riverside, and continues with his meaningless stride. He looks around for the giant bug, but it is nowhere to be seen.

It is a busy day in the city. The cars, trucks and bikes seem to run against each other, without any collision, and in the middle of all that, human beings try to stay alive. When the traffic light turns red, the vehicles come to a sudden halt, and Gregor crosses the road. Within a few seconds the light turns green. Gregor, already at the other side of the road, stands there idly, wondering where the insect will be. He soon finds it standing hesitant at the spot where he was, trying to cross the road and come towards him. The insect attempts to jump to his side, but the vehicles don't see this. They don't see it, instead run through the insect without care. Gregor sees the insect getting severed into two, and both the parts fly in different directions. Gregor looks at the scene with horror, without moving a bit. He instead turns back, and walks towards the railway station, as if nothing had happened.

CHAPTER FIFTY-ONE

Gregor exits the train and walks the lane that leads to his home. Although he is reluctant to go back to the prison, he knows he has to, because there is nowhere else he can be. At least in his house, at least for the time being, there's a bed he can sleep in, although it is locked from the outside. As he slowly walks the usual path in the evening, he sees a group of teenagers, probably the ones who usually cause menace, playing football in the middle of the road. Vehicles wait on either side, wait for the ball to be out of play. They seem afraid to ask the boys to let them pass. Gregor stays there, and watches them play. Moreover, he is in no hurry. The ball goes out, and they halt the play for a few seconds, to let the vehicles pass. It is a not a crowded street, so there were only a few vehicles. During the stoppage in play, Gregor walks up to one of the boys.

"Will you let me play?" He asks.

The boy looked at him in confusion. He turns back to his friends. "The man here wants to play with us. Can we let him in?" "We can," one of the others said. "There's already an absence of one man in your team. You can let him join." Gregor has never even properly seen a football in ten years, but he lets his intrusive thoughts win.

One of the boys explain to him the rules of the game, where the goal posts are, and also defined the opponents. The match starts. Gregor plays in the middle. He runs behind the opponents, trying to pick the ball from them. One of them makes a miss pass and it reaches under Gregor's foot. He tries to dribble with it, pushing the boys away, and one of them lands a sliding tackle on him, and Gregor falls down on the metalled road. Gregor's team claims that it is a penalty. With the halt in the play, the vehicles pass through. A rule of the game was such that the person who wins the penalty should take it. After the vehicles pass through, and the match resumes, Gregor prepares himself before the goal for taking his penalty. The keeper is ready to defend the goal. He makes a small run and kicks the ball. The ball flies with power and elevation and lands inside a shop, by the roadside.

"It's better if you don't play," one of the boys says.

Gregor nods, and walks out of the football area.

When he reaches a spot where no one is noticing him, he puts his hand inside the pocket and takes out the white rose O gave him by the riverside. It is all soiled and the peduncle is broken. Two of the petals fall out, and Gregor prevents the fall with his other hand. He looks at the flower and the petals and thinks about O, and the moments they spent together by the river side, the way she told him her story, how her face looked as if she was fed up with her tears, how the police officers retrieved her unconscious, and woke her up, with the first aid methods, how they handcuffed her and led her to the police vehicle, how she looked at him for the last time, before entering into the vehicle. Gregor stands there, looking at the flower as if he is frozen in time.

He then takes his mobile phone, and calls his cousin, who takes the phone within a few rings.

"I met a girl, who happened to kill someone, and she seemed so mentally disturbed. Is there any way I can let her out?" He tells her right away.

"Where are you and what the hell are you upto?"

"I'm at home."

"Can you come to my place now? If you are free?" She asks him. "We can sit down and talk, and don't you have work today?"

"I will tell you about that when I come to your place. Also, I want to know about the therapist you told me about, the other day."

"Sure. Come to my place. I will send you the location. I will be free till 7 in the evening. After that I will return home in the 9 PM flight," she says.

"Alright, I'm coming then," Gregor says and cuts the call.

He walks back. A lonely man, but with a rose in his hand.